THE Three Little PIGS

WRITTEN BY STEPHANIE PETERS

ILLUSTRATED BY CÉSAR SAMANIEGO

PICTURE WINDOW BOOKS
a capstone imprint

Published by Picture Window Books,
an imprint of Capstone
1710 Roe Crest Drive
North Mankato, Minnesota 56003
capstonepub.com

Library of Congress Cataloging-in-Publication Data
Names: Peters, Stephanie True, 1965– author. | Samaniego, César,
    1975– illustrator.
Title: The three little pigs / by Stephanie Peters ; illustrated by César
    Samaniego.
Other titles: Three little pigs. English.
Description: North Mankato, Minnesota : Picture Window Books, an
    imprint of Capstone, [2022] | Series: A Discover Graphics fairy tale |
    Audience: Ages 5–7. | Audience: Grades K–1. | Summary: Three little
    pigs build their own homes and encounter a threatening wolf.
Identifiers: LCCN 2021006142 (print) | LCCN 2021006143 (ebook) |
    ISBN 9781663914132 (hardcover) | ISBN 9781663921437 (paperback) |
    ISBN 9781663914293 (ebook pdf)
Subjects: LCSH: Graphic novels. | CYAC: Graphic novels. | Pigs—
    Fiction. | Dwellings—Design and construction—Fiction.
Classification: LCC PZ7.7.P44 Th 2022 (print) | LCC PZ7.7.P44 (ebook) |
    DDC 741.5/973—dc23
LC record available at https://lccn.loc.gov/2021006142
LC ebook record available at https://lccn.loc.gov/2021006143

Designed by Kay Fraser

WORDS TO KNOW

build—to make by putting together parts or
materials

chore—a small job that needs to be done
regularly

straw—dry plant stems

Printed and bound in China. PO4911

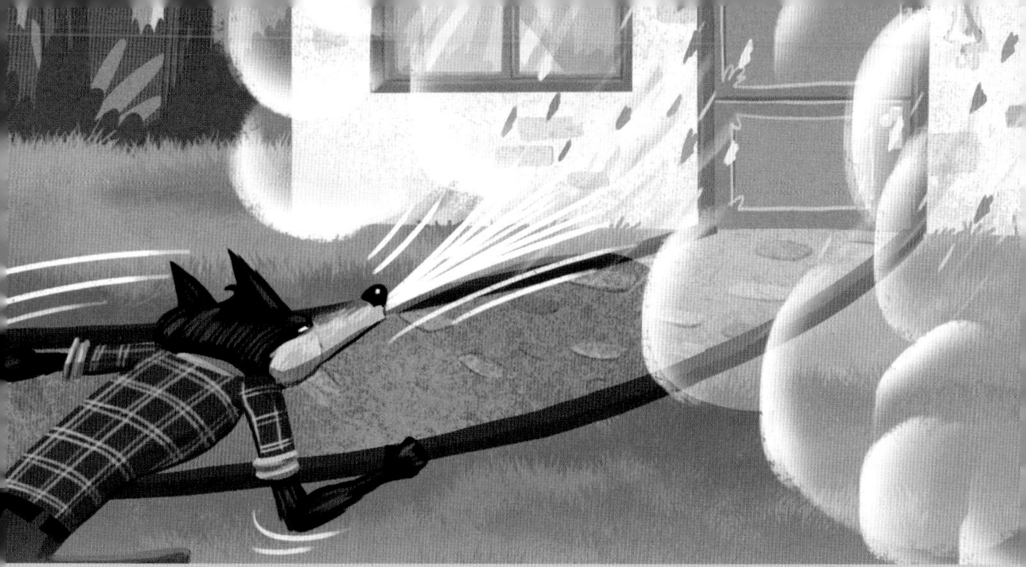

CAST OF CHARACTERS

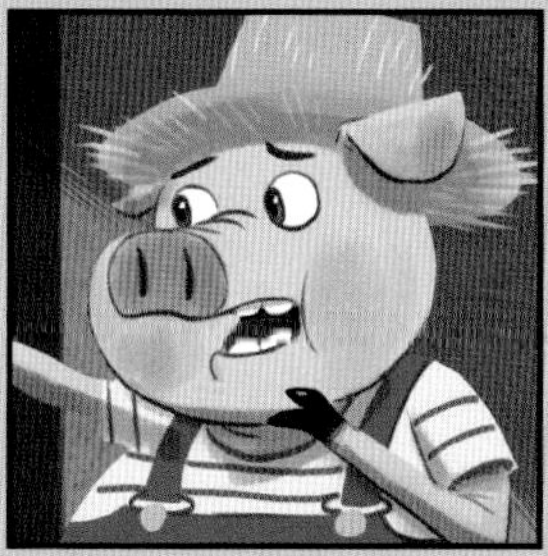

Jem builds his house out of straw.

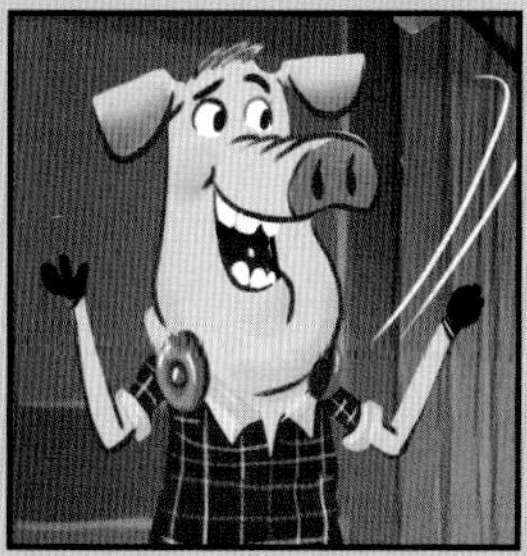

Clem builds his house out of sticks.

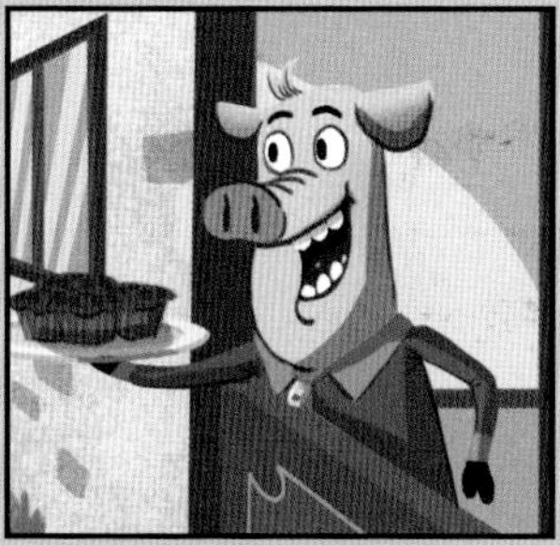

Bo is hardworking. He builds his house out of bricks.

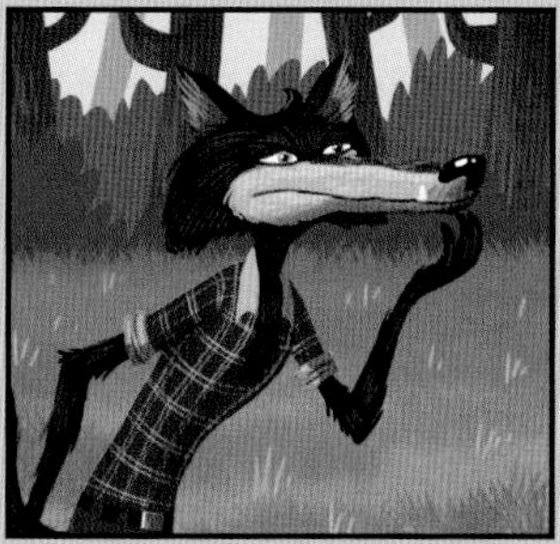

The **big bad wolf** is hungry. He chases after the pigs and tries to destroy their houses.

HOW TO READ
A GRAPHIC NOVEL

Graphic novels are easy to read. Boxes called panels show you how to follow the story. Look at the panels from left to right and top to bottom.

Read the word boxes and word balloons from left to right as well. Don't forget the sound and action words in the pictures.

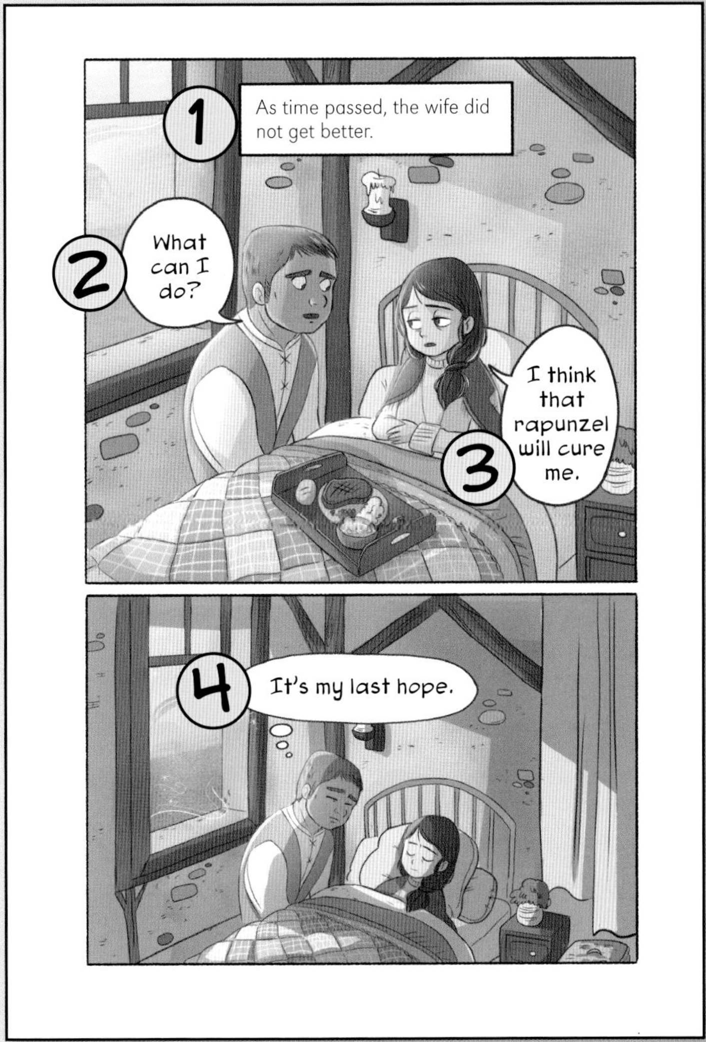
1
As time passed, the wife did not get better.
2
What can I do?
3
I think that rapunzel will cure me.
4
It's my last hope.

The pictures and the words work together to tell the whole story.

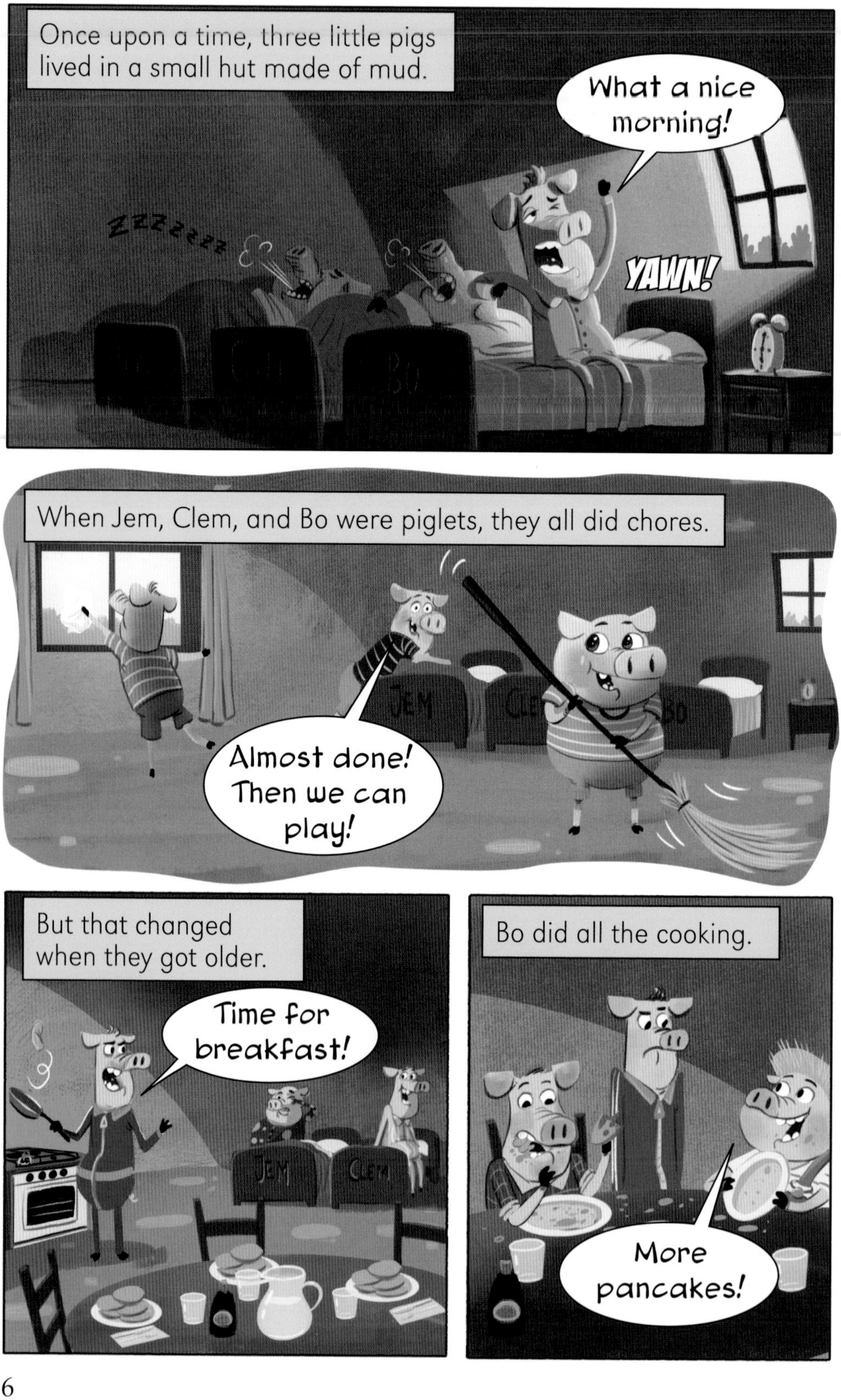
Once upon a time, three little pigs lived in a small hut made of mud.
What a nice morning!
YAWN!
When Jem, Clem, and Bo were piglets, they all did chores.
Almost done! Then we can play!
But that changed when they got older.
Time for breakfast!
Bo did all the cooking.
More pancakes!

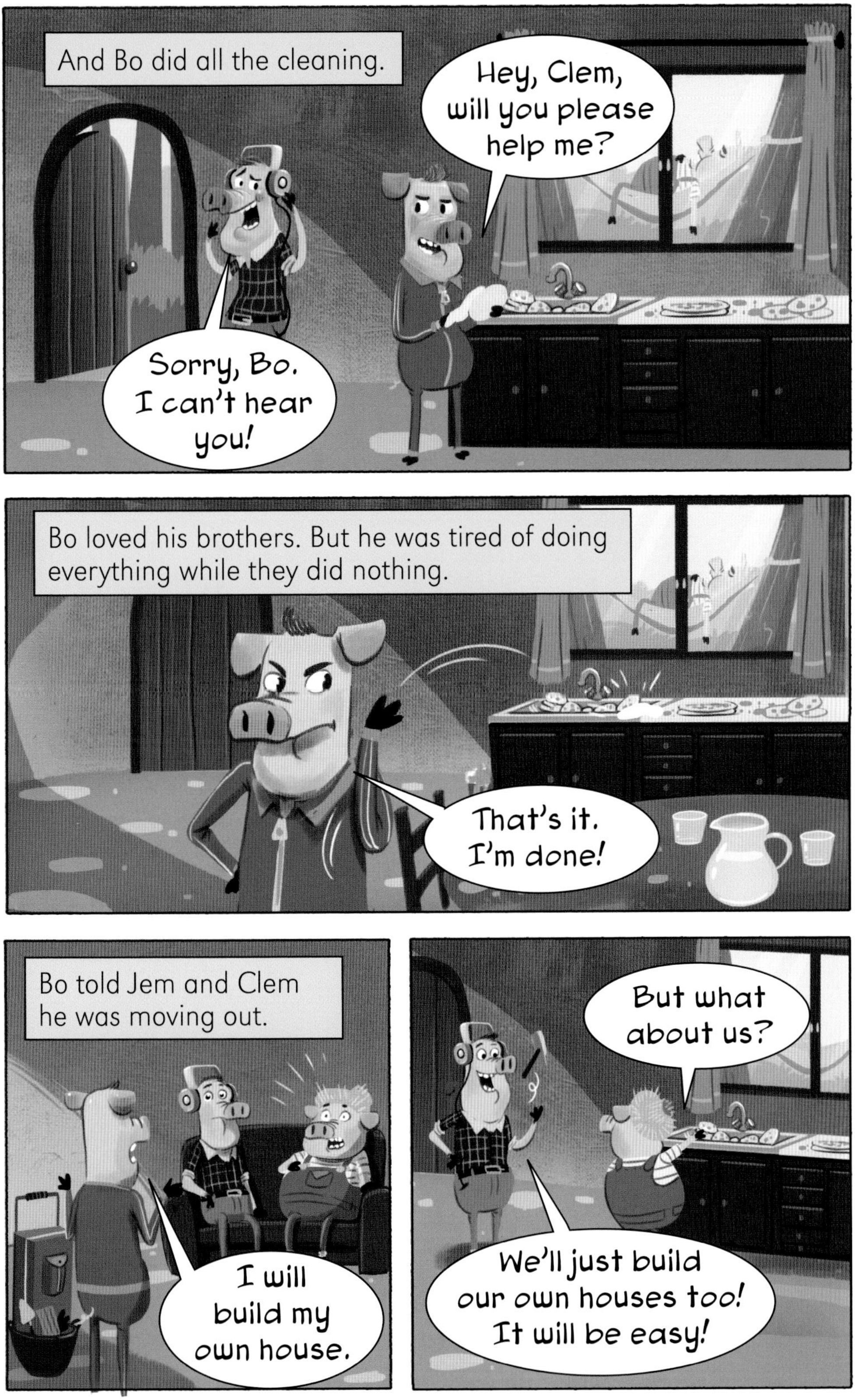
And Bo did all the cleaning.
Hey, Clem, will you please help me?
Sorry, Bo. I can't hear you!
Bo loved his brothers. But he was tired of doing everything while they did nothing.
That's it. I'm done!
Bo told Jem and Clem he was moving out.
I will build my own house.
But what about us?
We'll just build our own houses too! It will be easy!

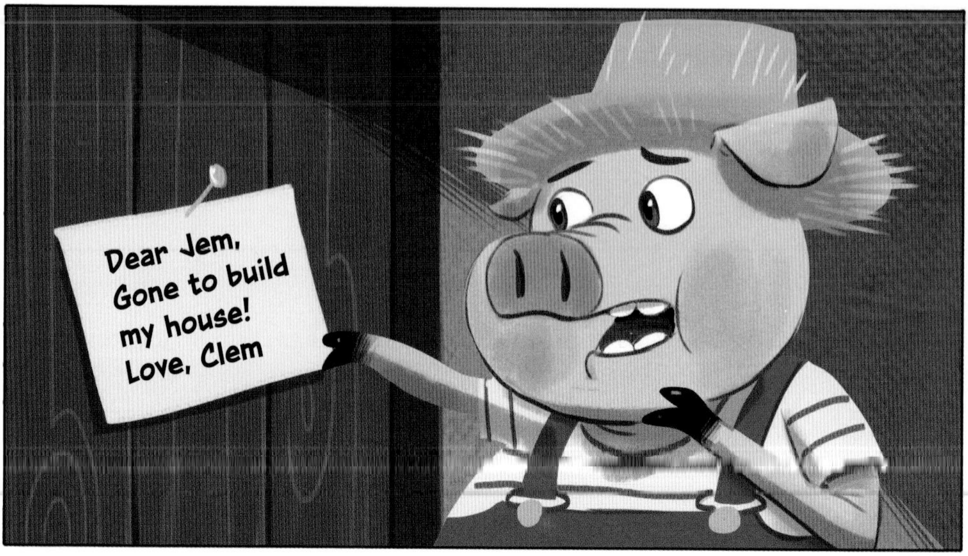
Dear Jem,
Gone to build my house!
Love, Clem

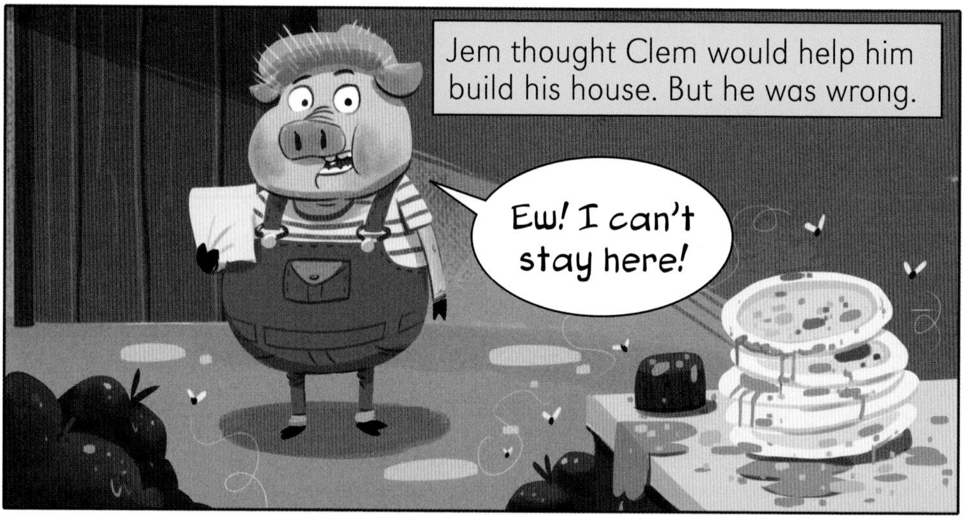
Jem thought Clem would help him build his house. But he was wrong.
Ew! I can't stay here!

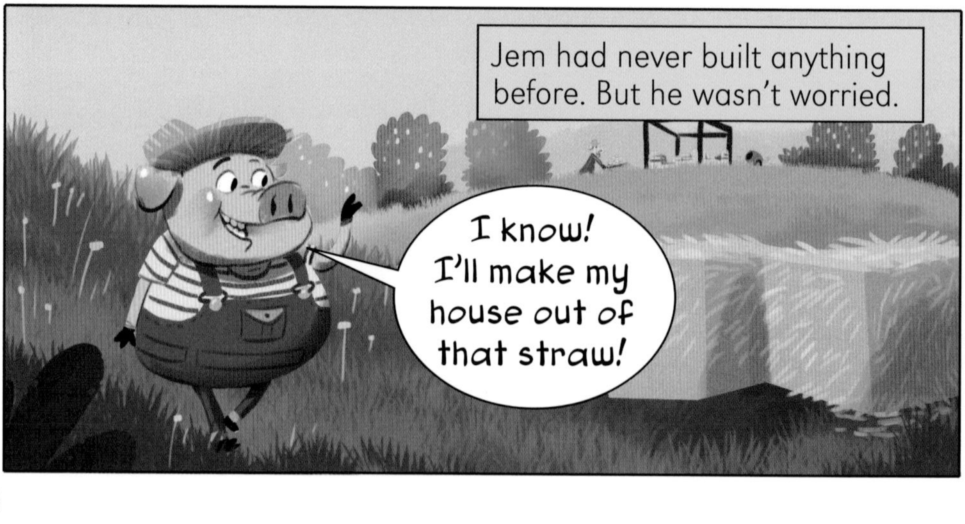
Jem had never built anything before. But he wasn't worried.
I know! I'll make my house out of that straw!

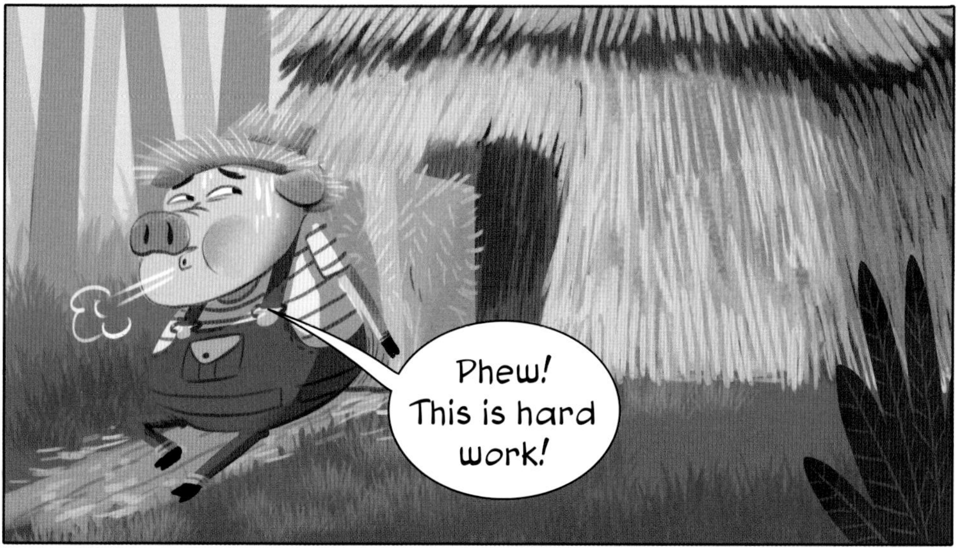
Phew!
This is hard work!

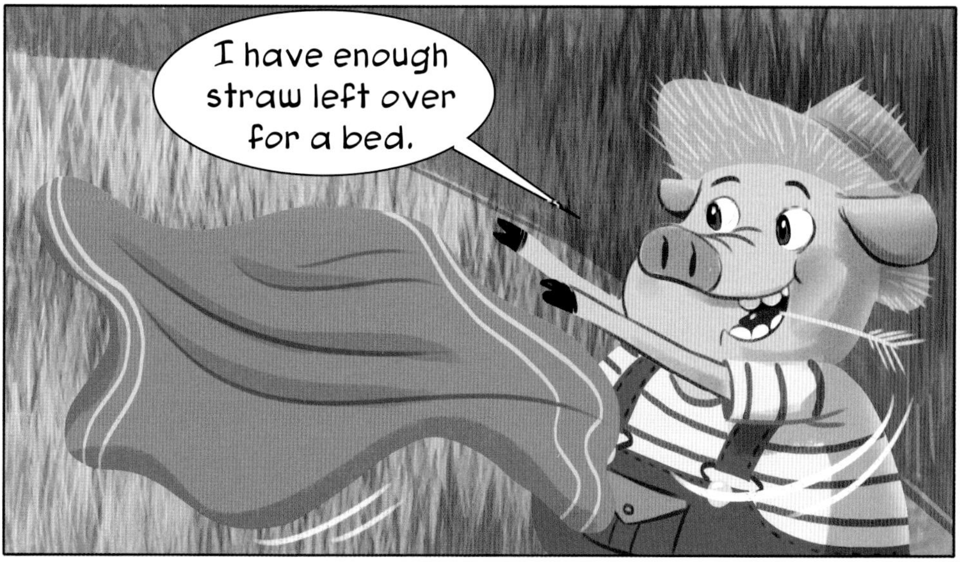
I have enough straw left over for a bed.

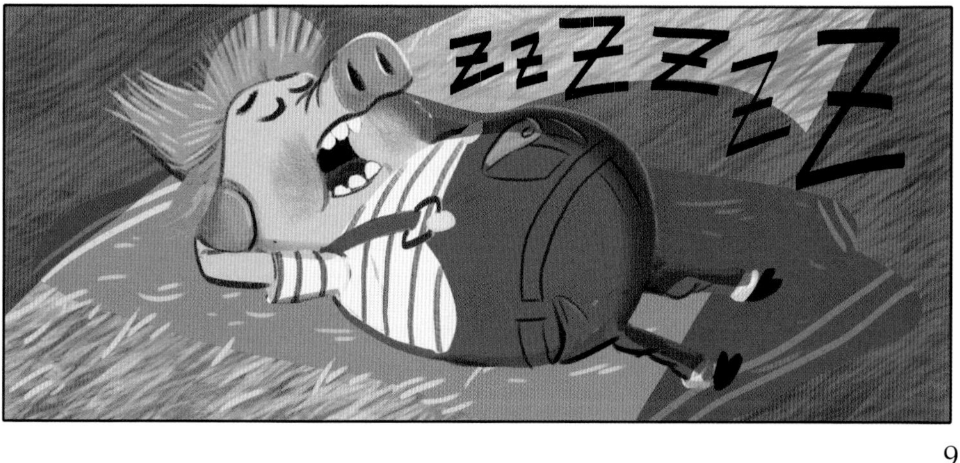
ZzZZZzZZ

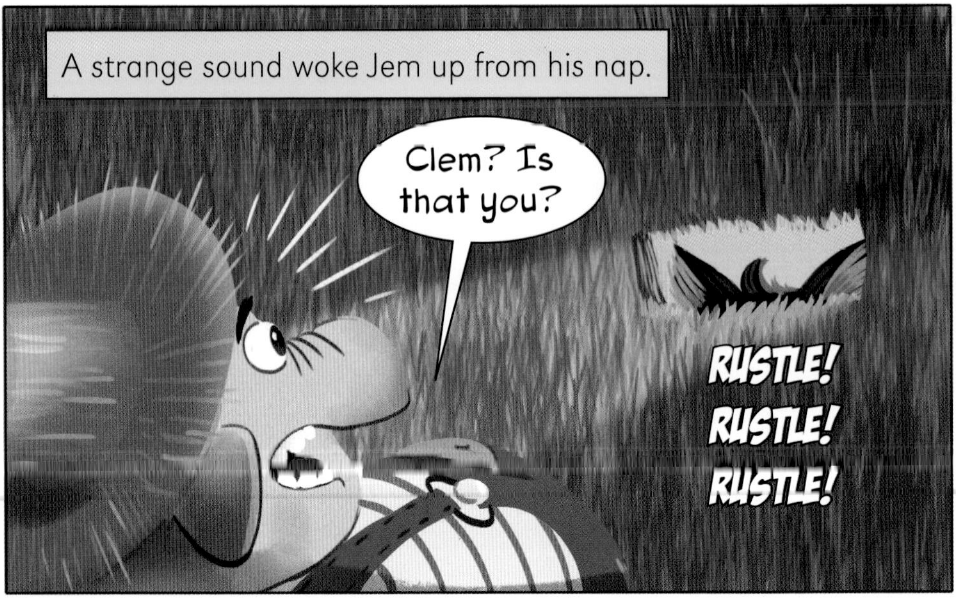
A strange sound woke Jem up from his nap.
Clem? Is that you?
RUSTLE! RUSTLE! RUSTLE!

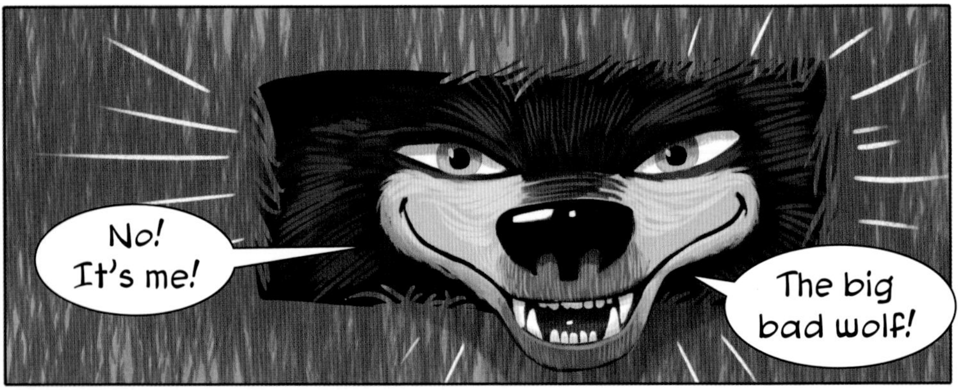
No! It's me!
The big bad wolf!

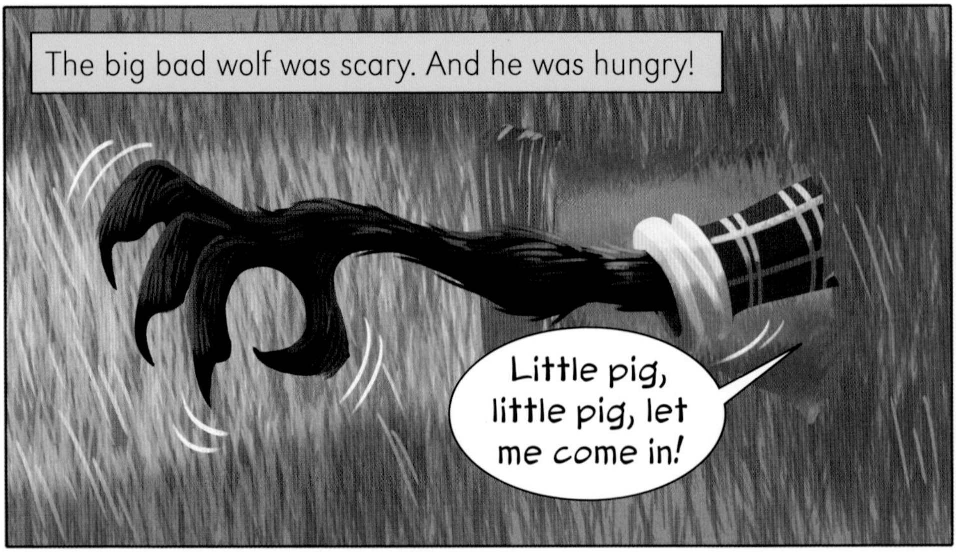
The big bad wolf was scary. And he was hungry!
Little pig, little pig, let me come in!

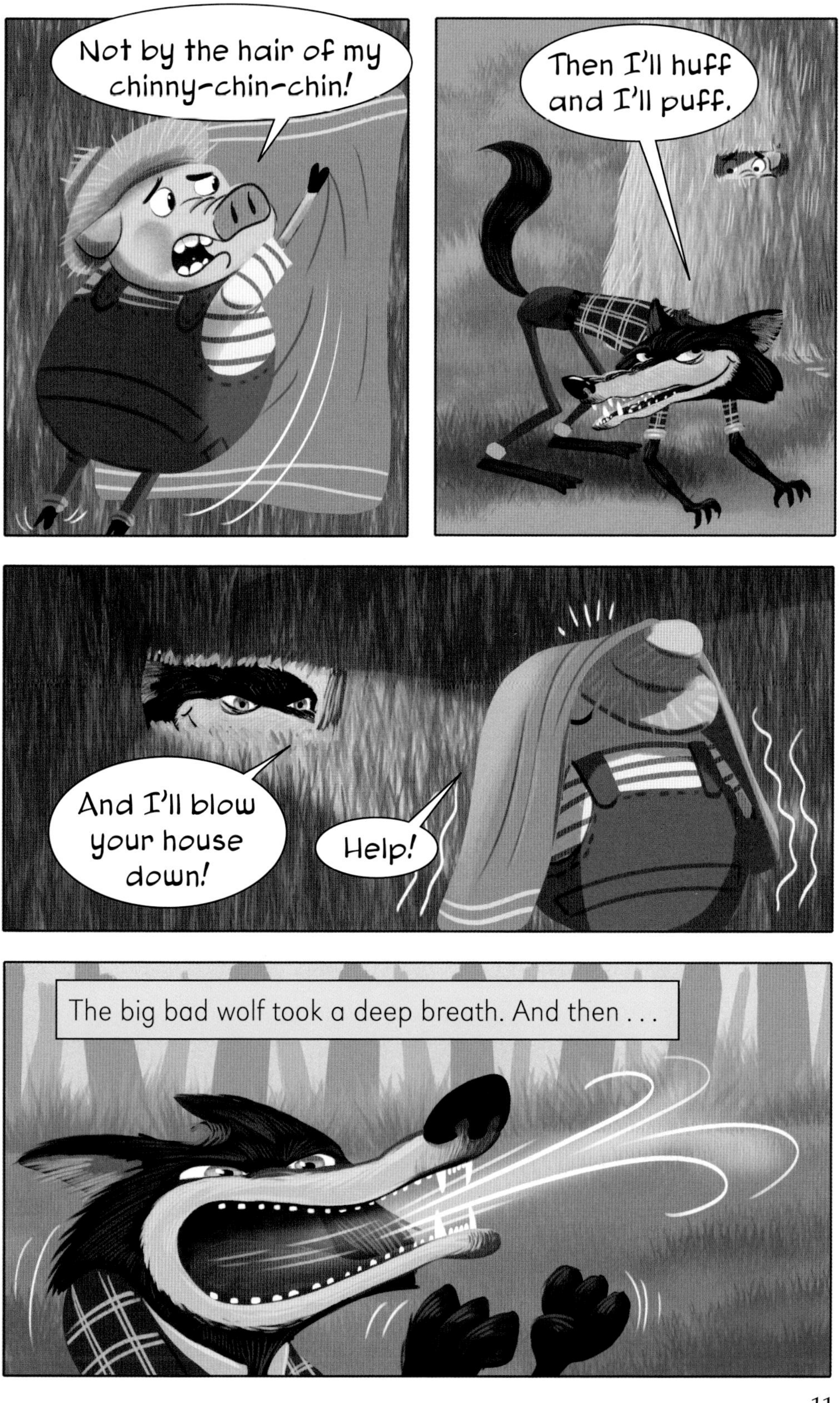
Not by the hair of my chinny-chin-chin!
Then I'll huff and I'll puff.
And I'll blow your house down!
Help!
The big bad wolf took a deep breath. And then . . .

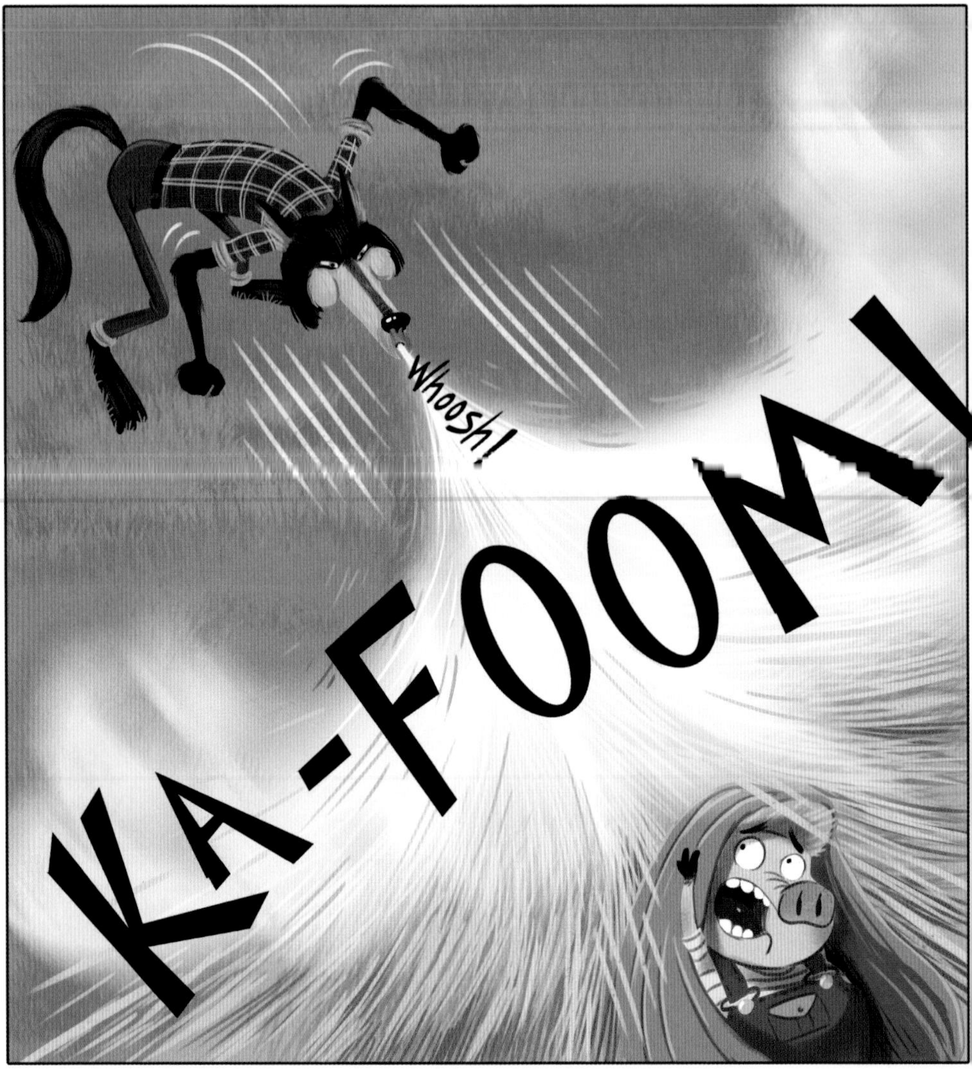
Whoosh!
KA-FOOM!

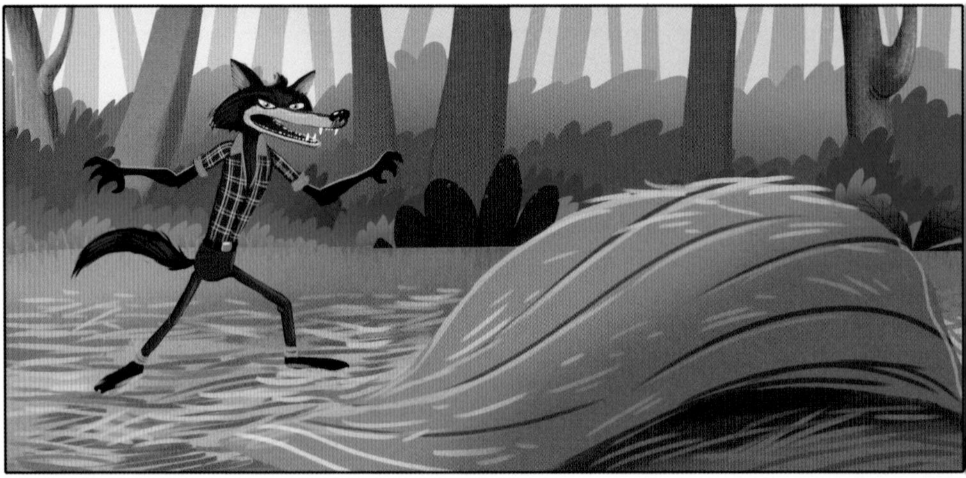

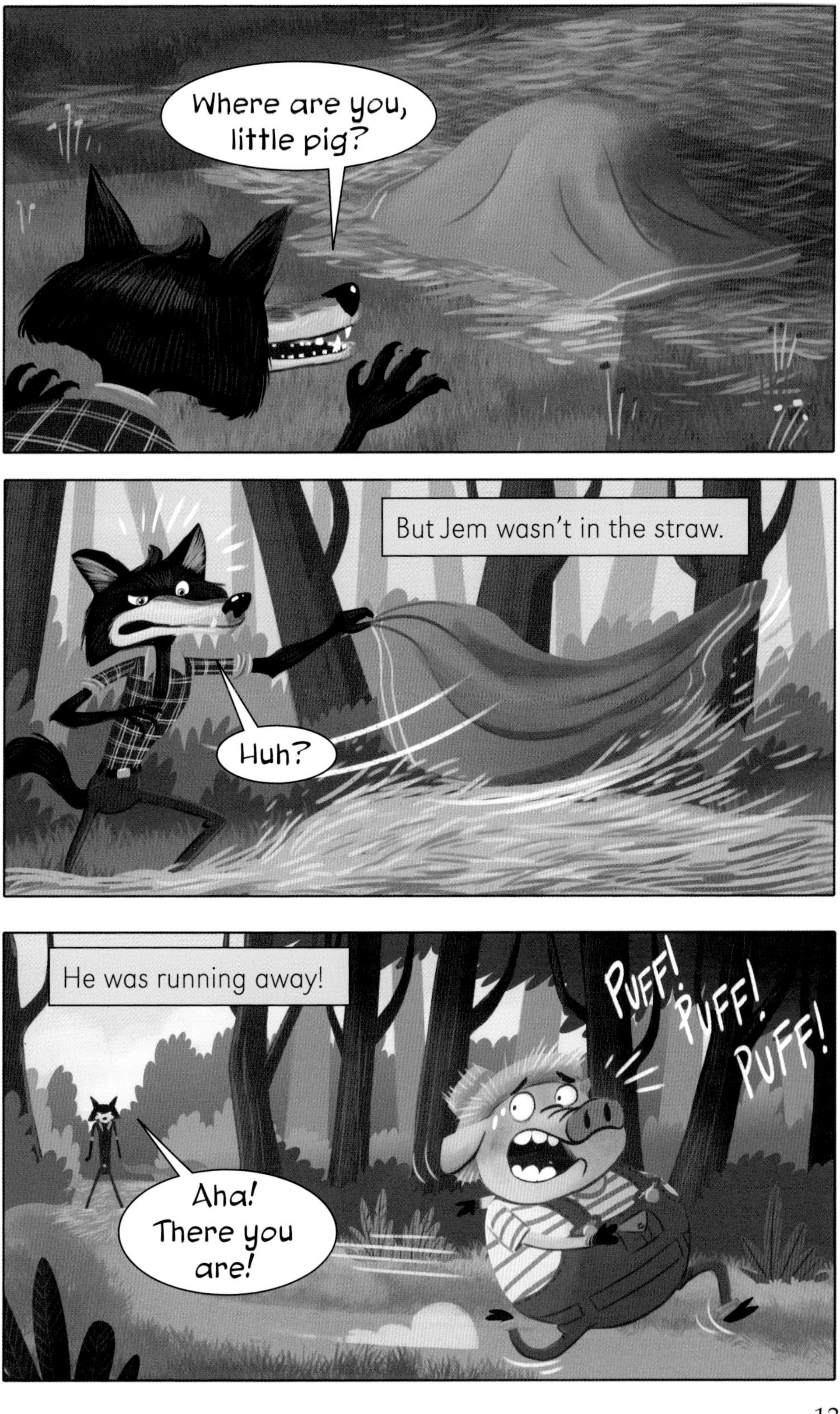
Where are you, little pig?
But Jem wasn't in the straw.
Huh?
He was running away!
PUFF! PUFF! PUFF!
Aha! There you are!

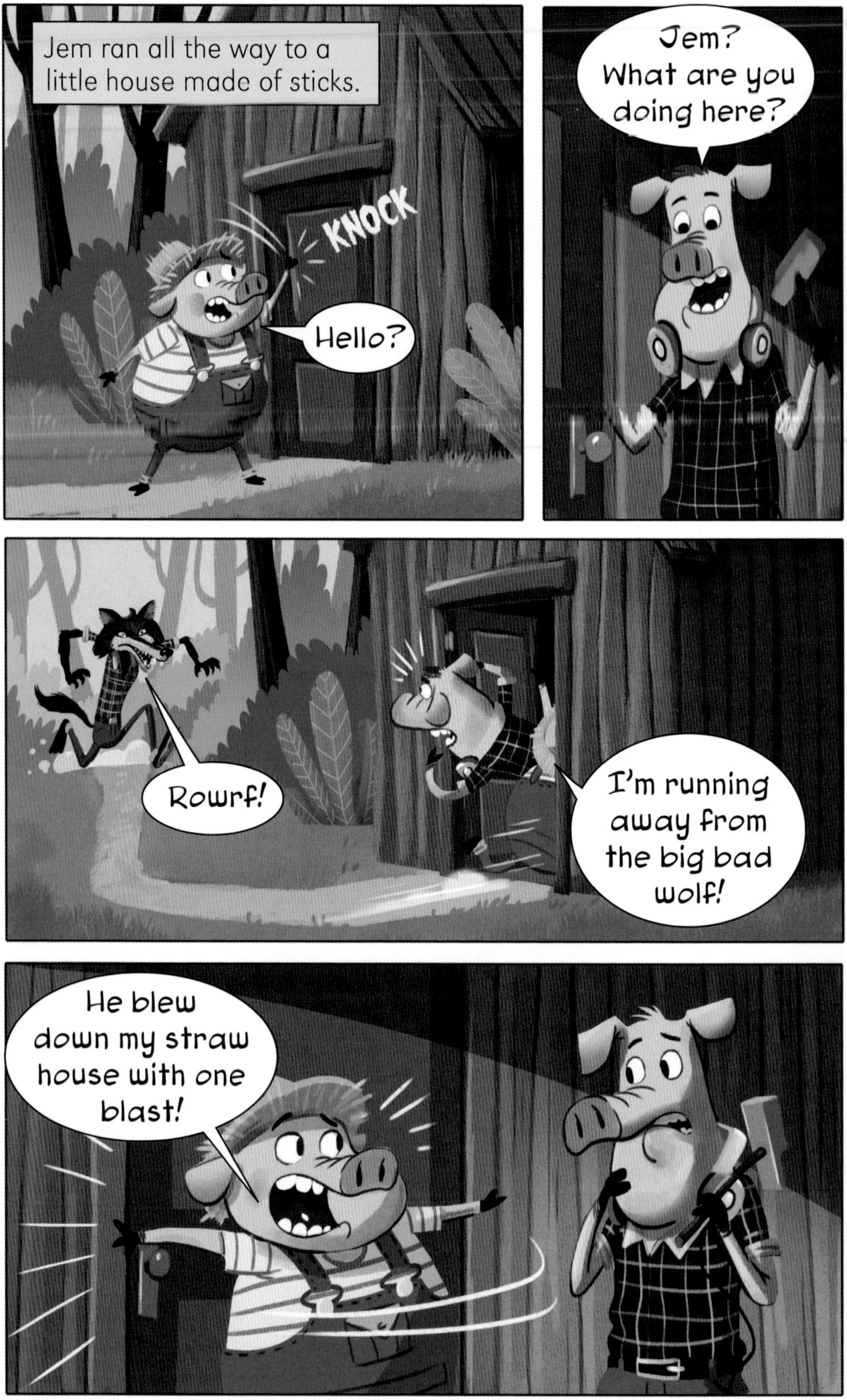
Jem ran all the way to a little house made of sticks.
KNOCK
Hello?
Jem? What are you doing here?
Rowrf!
I'm running away from the big bad wolf!
He blew down my straw house with one blast!

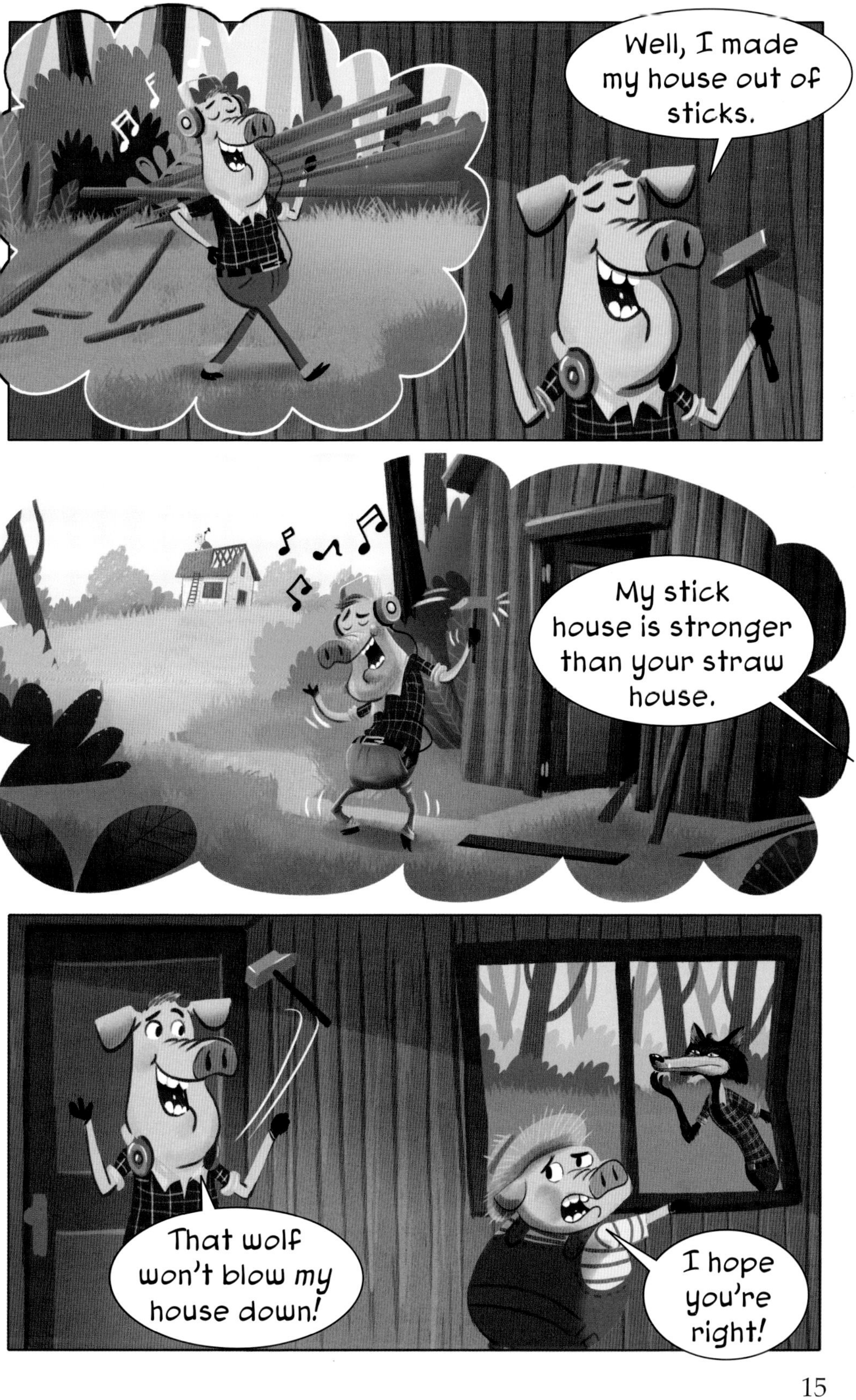
Well, I made my house out of sticks.
My stick house is stronger than your straw house.
That wolf won't blow my house down!
I hope you're right!

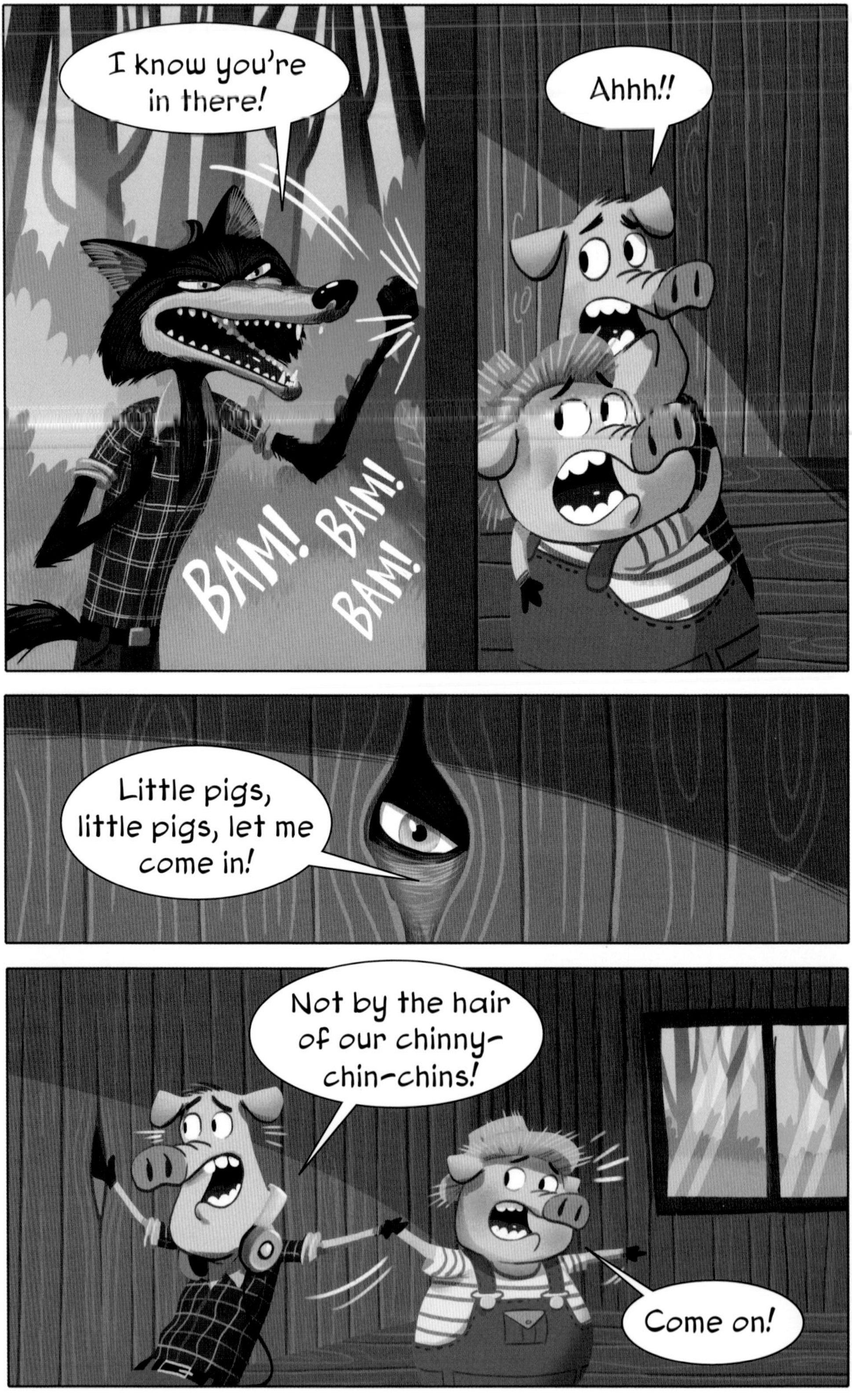
I know you're in there!
BAM! BAM! BAM!
Ahhh!!
Little pigs, little pigs, let me come in!
Not by the hair of our chinny-chin-chins!
Come on!

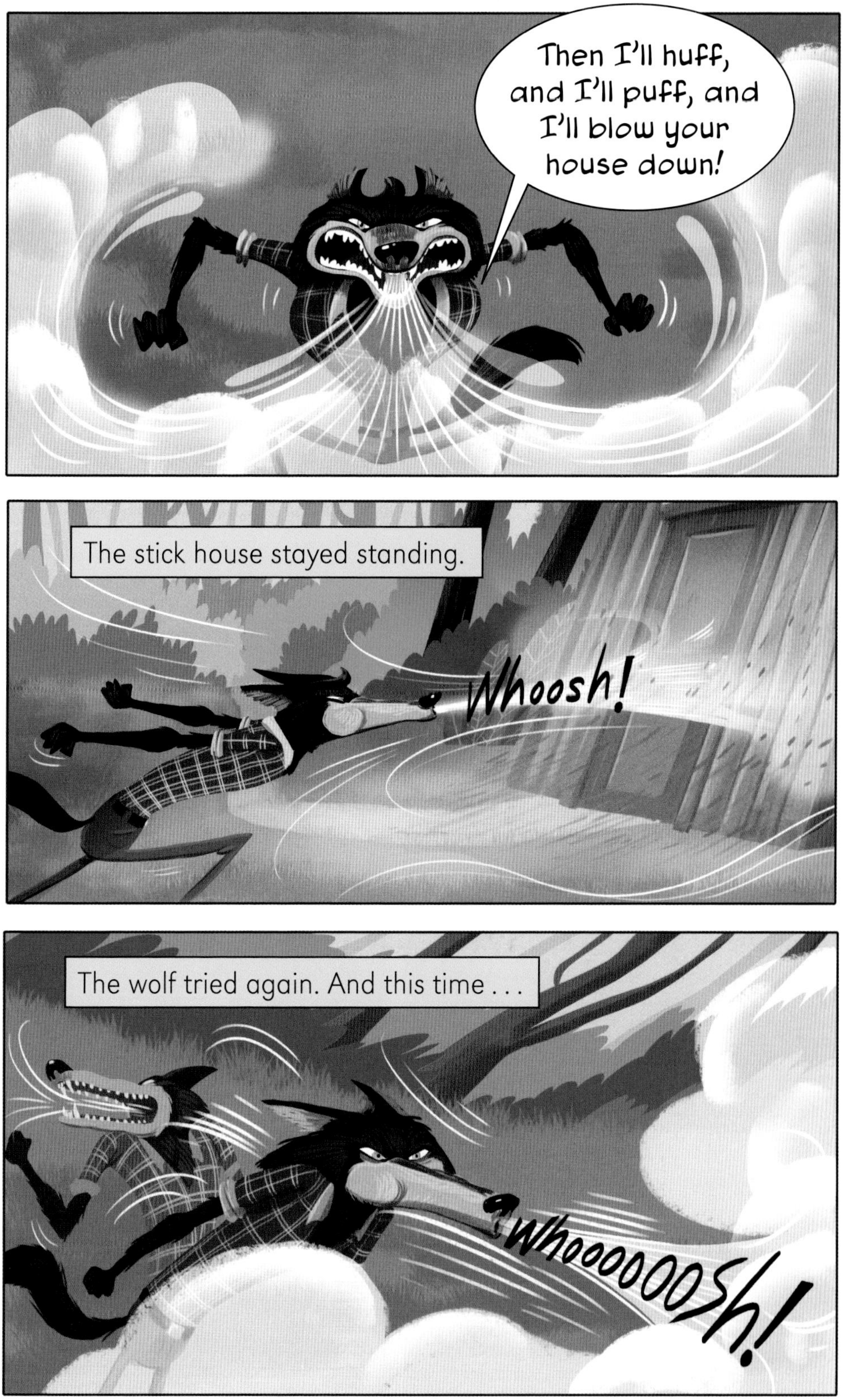
Then I'll huff, and I'll puff, and I'll blow your house down!
The stick house stayed standing.
Whoosh!
The wolf tried again. And this time . . .
Whoooooosh!

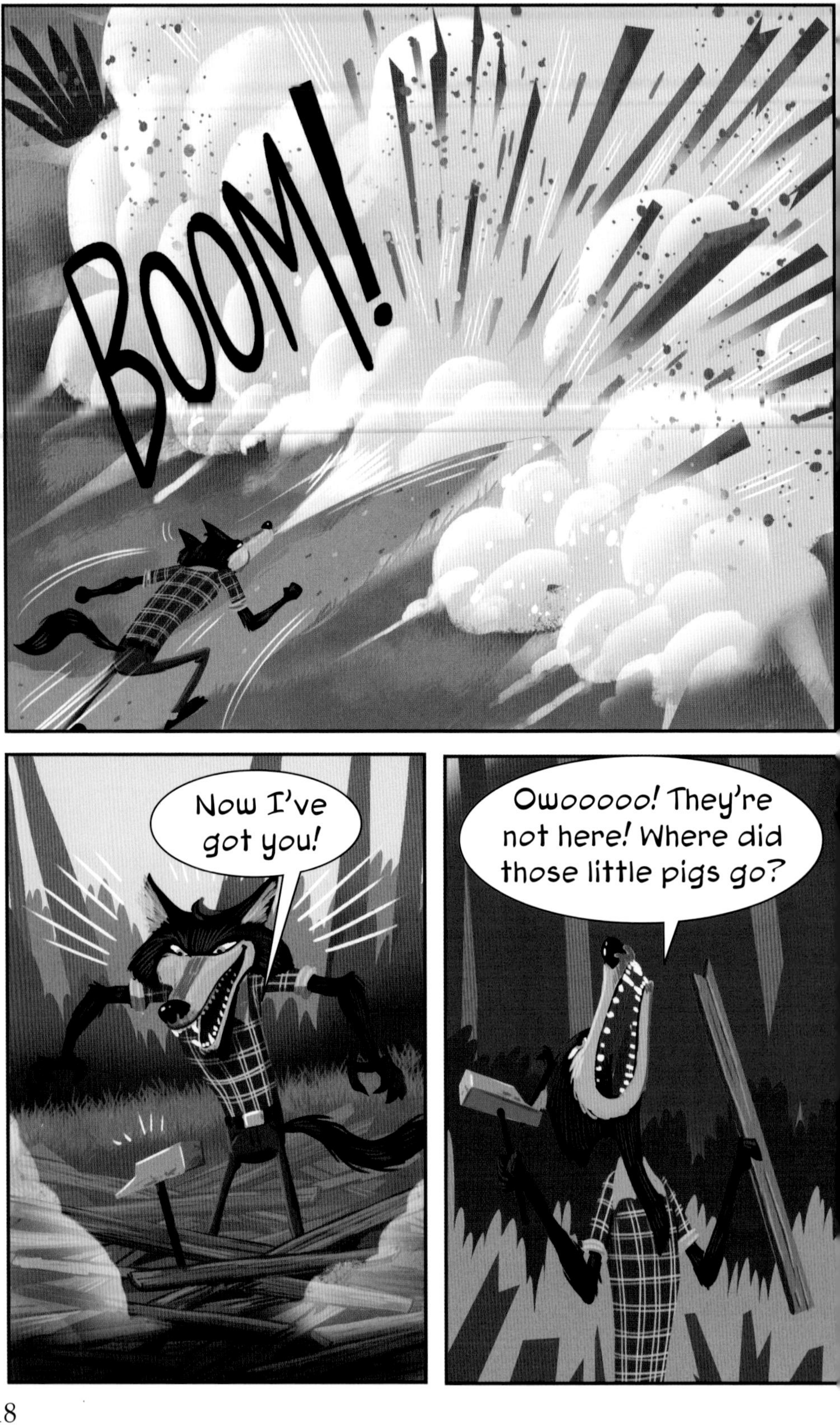
BOOM!
Now I've got you!
Owooooo! They're not here! Where did those little pigs go?

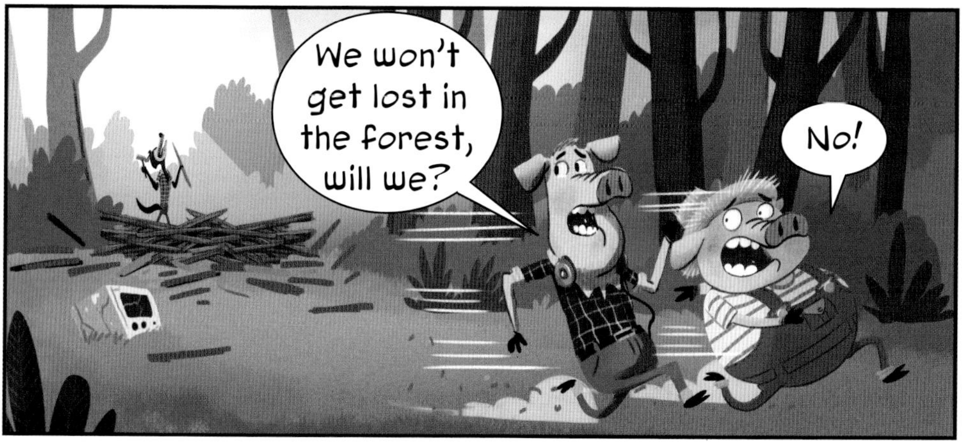
We won't get lost in the forest, will we?
No!

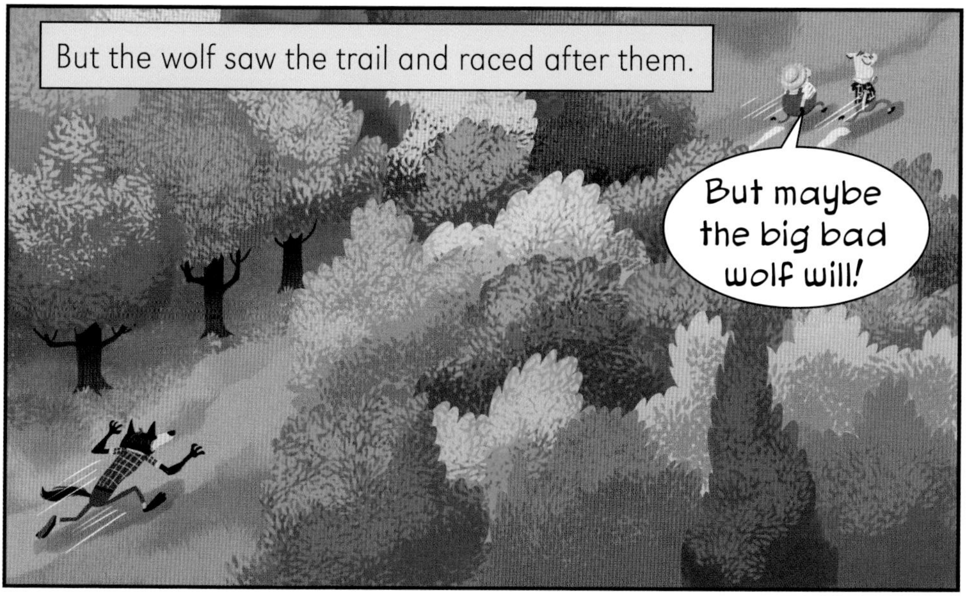
But the wolf saw the trail and raced after them.
But maybe the big bad wolf will!

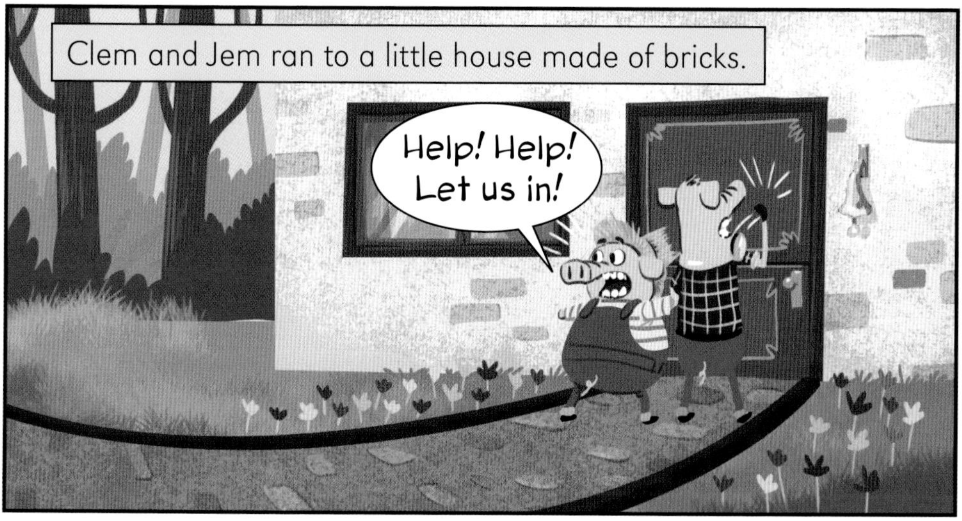
Clem and Jem ran to a little house made of bricks.
Help! Help! Let us in!

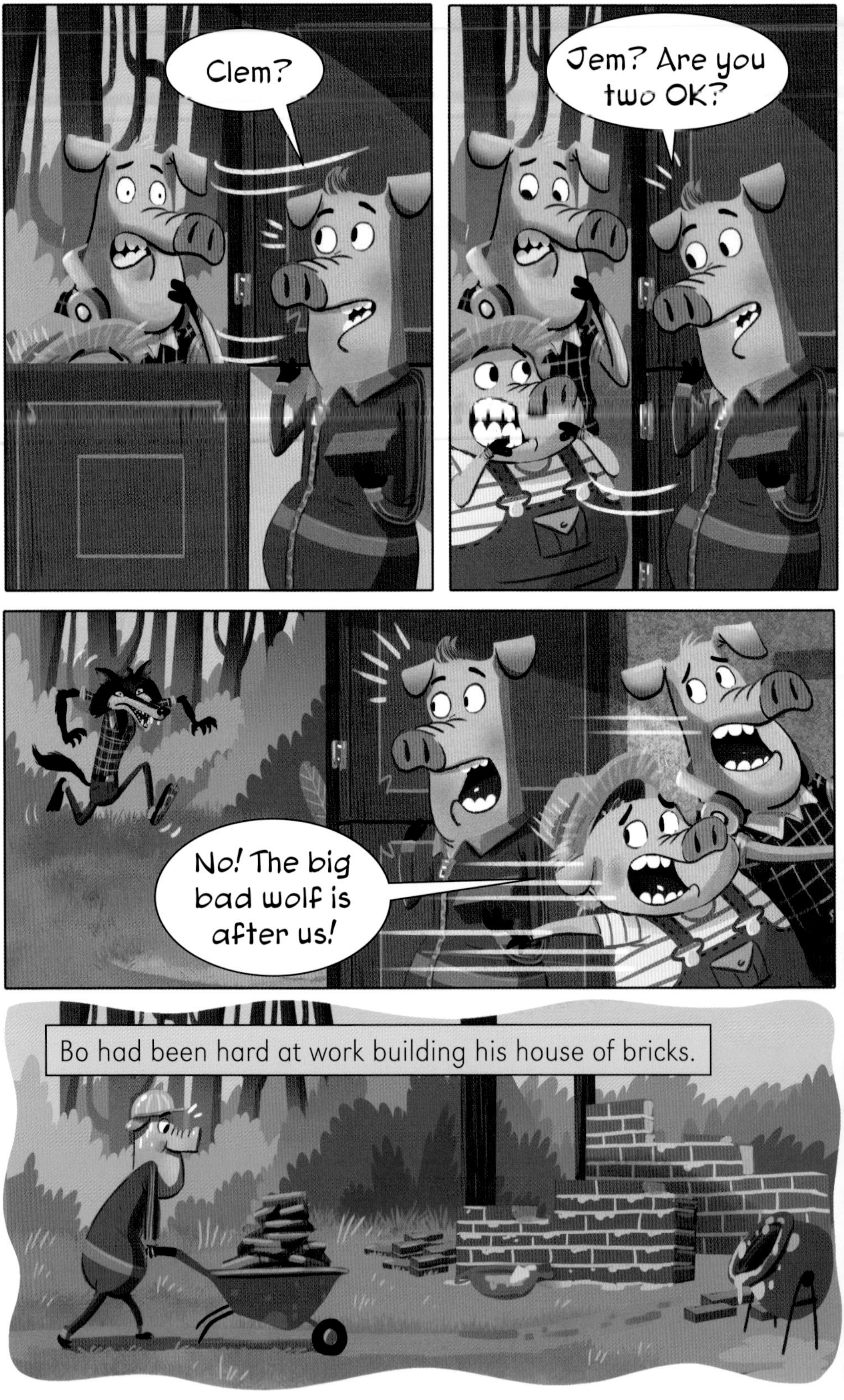
Clem?
Jem? Are you two OK?
No! The big bad wolf is after us!
Bo had been hard at work building his house of bricks.

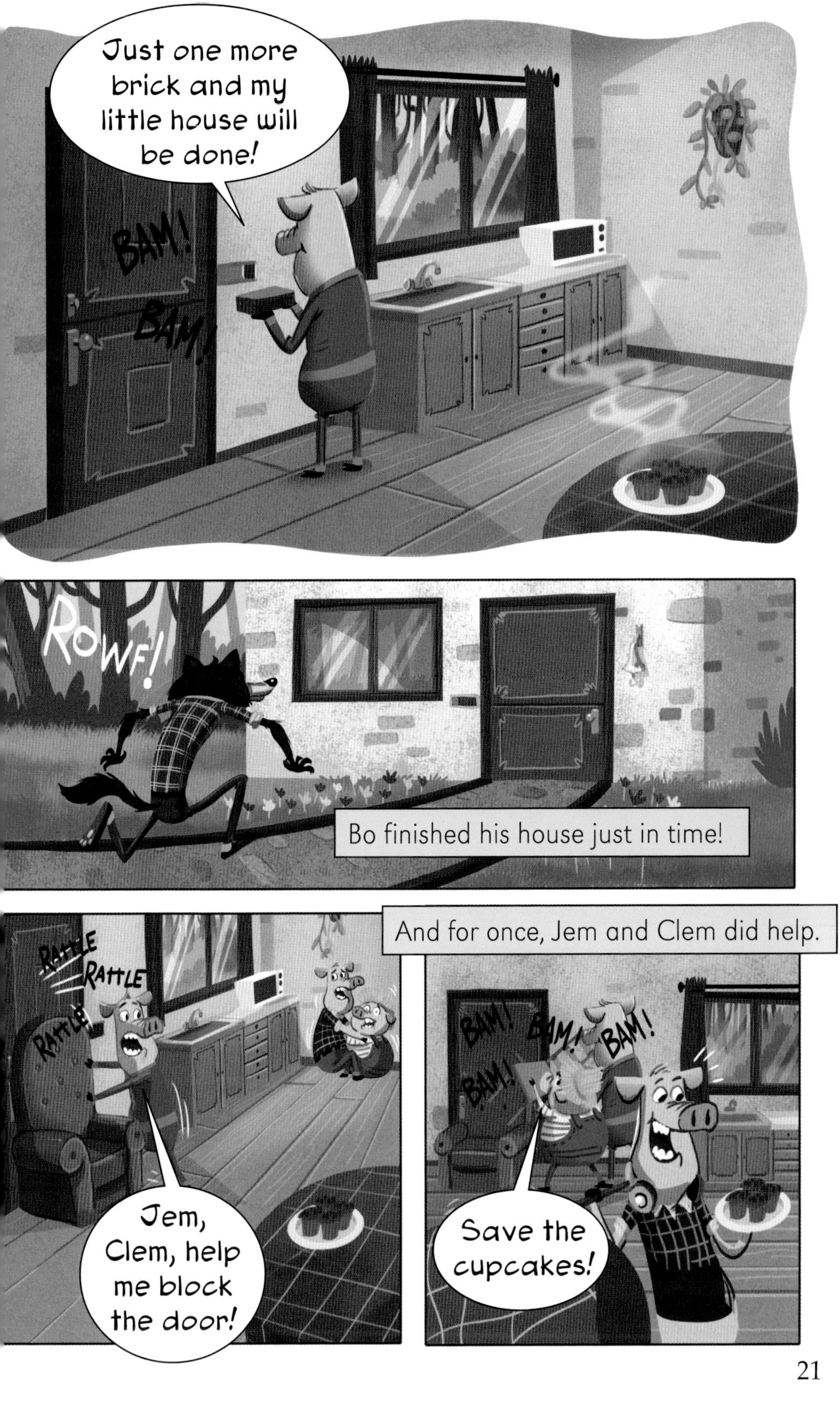
Just one more brick and my little house will be done!
BAM!
BAM!
ROWF!
Bo finished his house just in time!
And for once, Jem and Clem did help.
RATTLE
RATTLE
RATTLE
Jem, Clem, help me block the door!
BAM!
BAM!
BAM!
BAM!
Save the cupcakes!

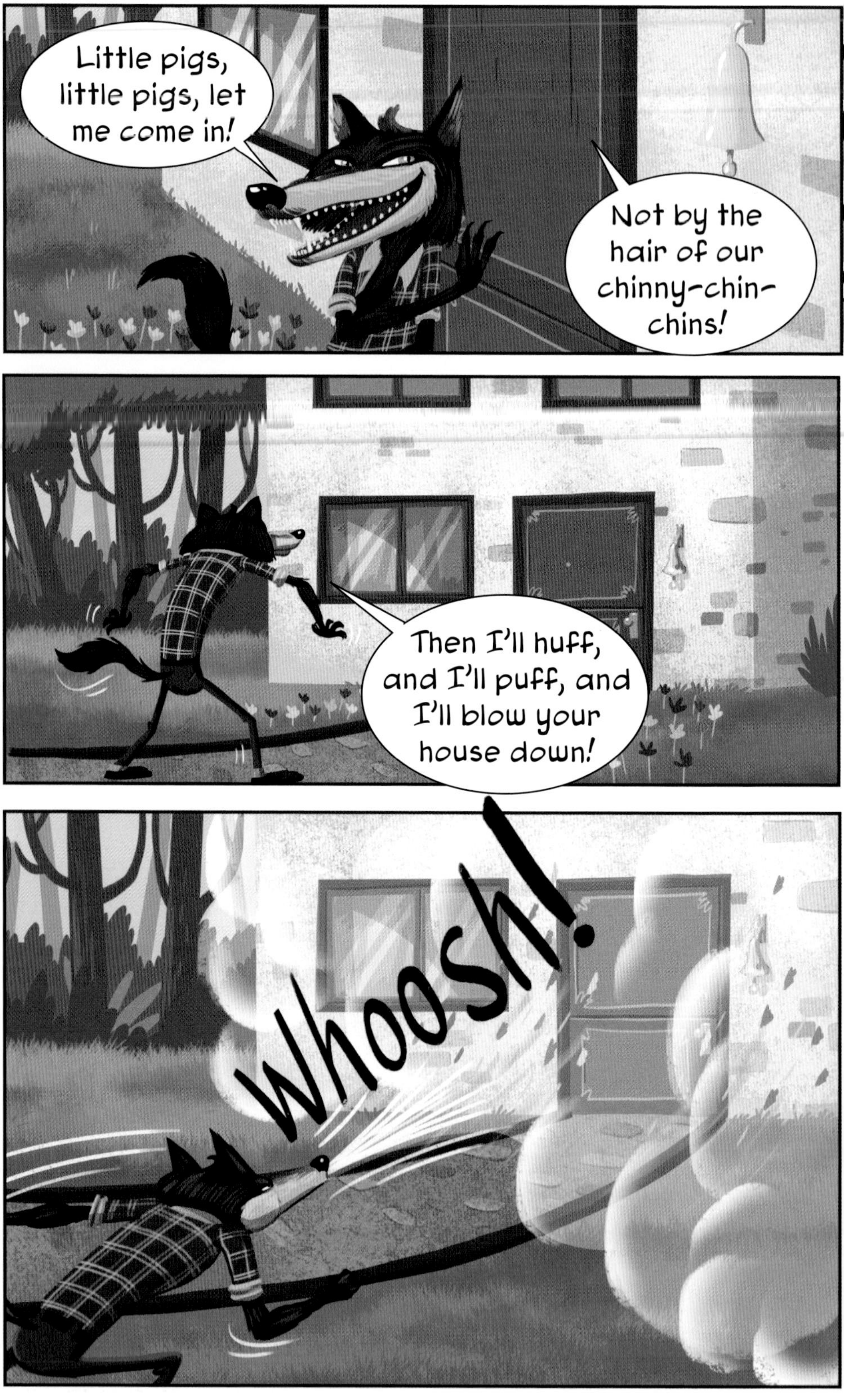
Little pigs, little pigs, let me come in!
Not by the hair of our chinny-chin-chins!
Then I'll huff, and I'll puff, and I'll blow your house down!
Whoosh!

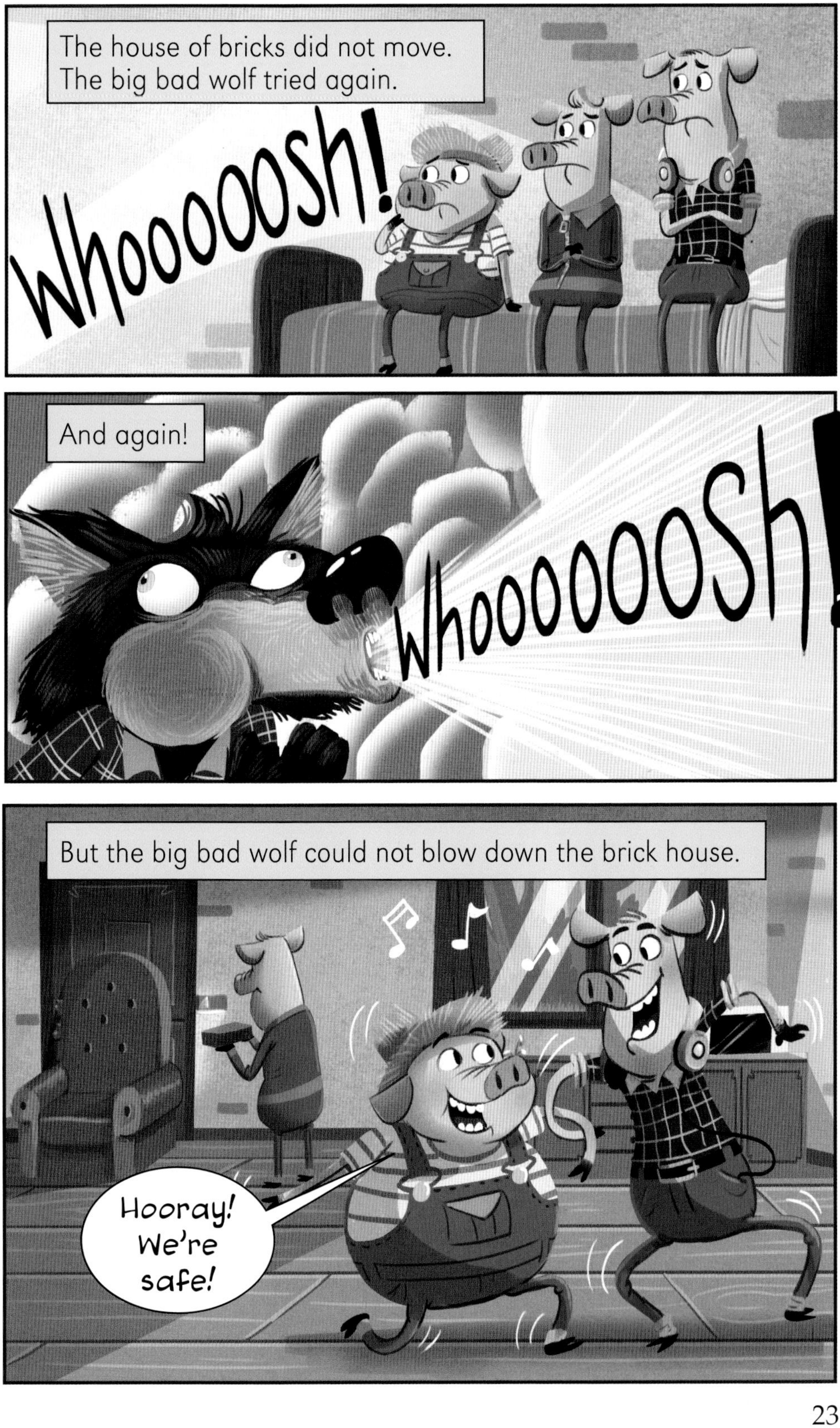
The house of bricks did not move.
The big bad wolf tried again.
Whooooosh!
And again!
Whoooooosh!
But the big bad wolf could not blow down the brick house.
Hooray! We're safe!

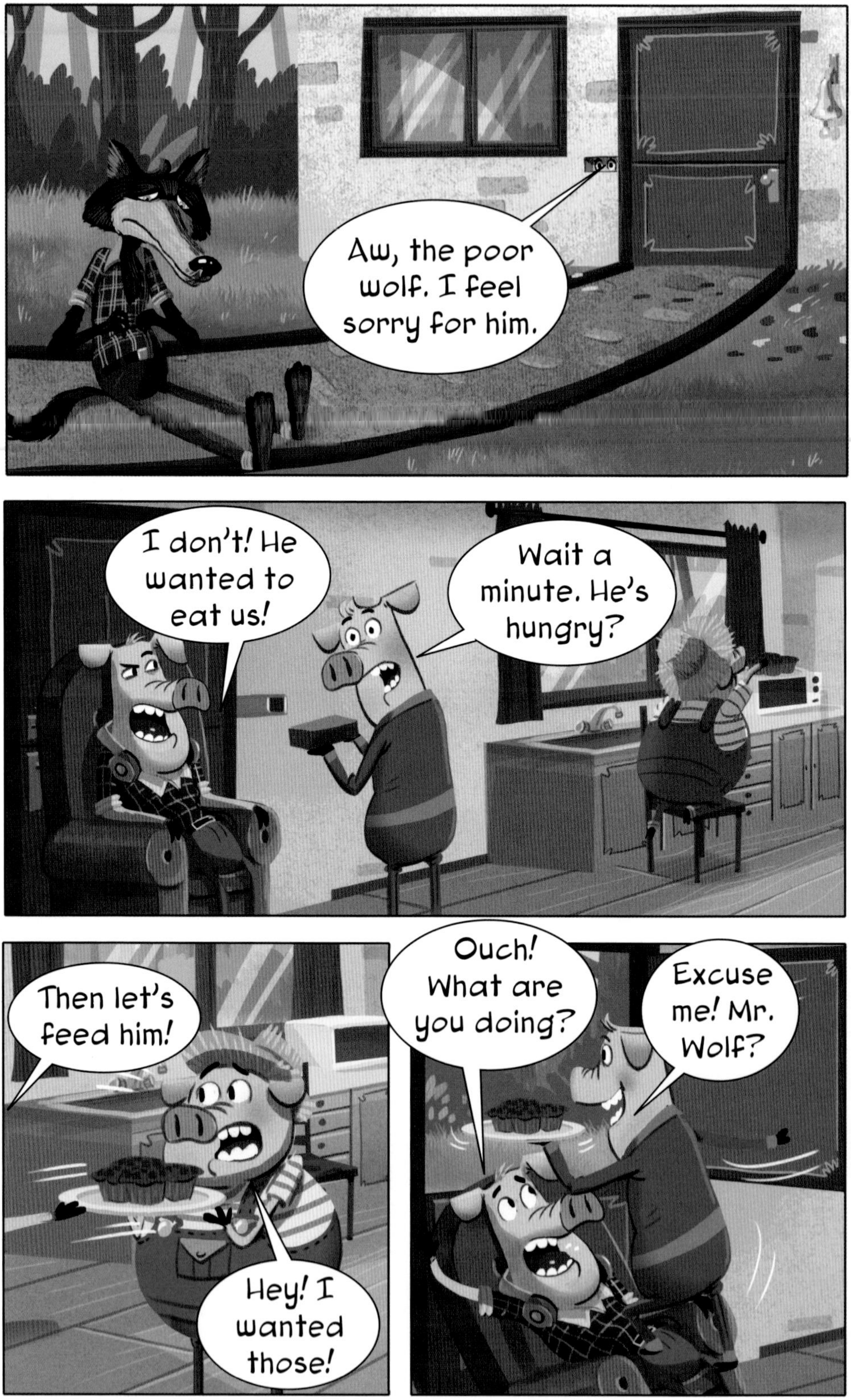
Aw, the poor wolf. I feel sorry for him.
I don't! He wanted to eat us!
Wait a minute. He's hungry?
Then let's feed him!
Hey! I wanted those!
Ouch! What are you doing?
Excuse me! Mr. Wolf?

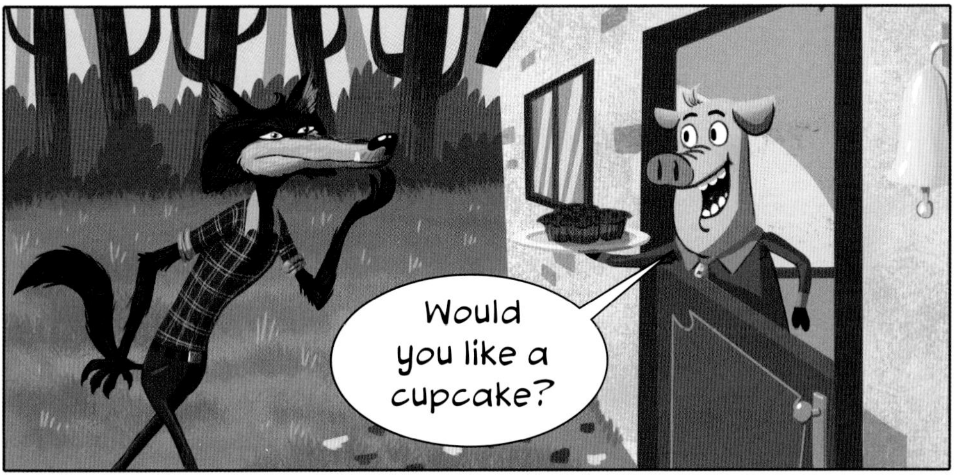
Would you like a cupcake?

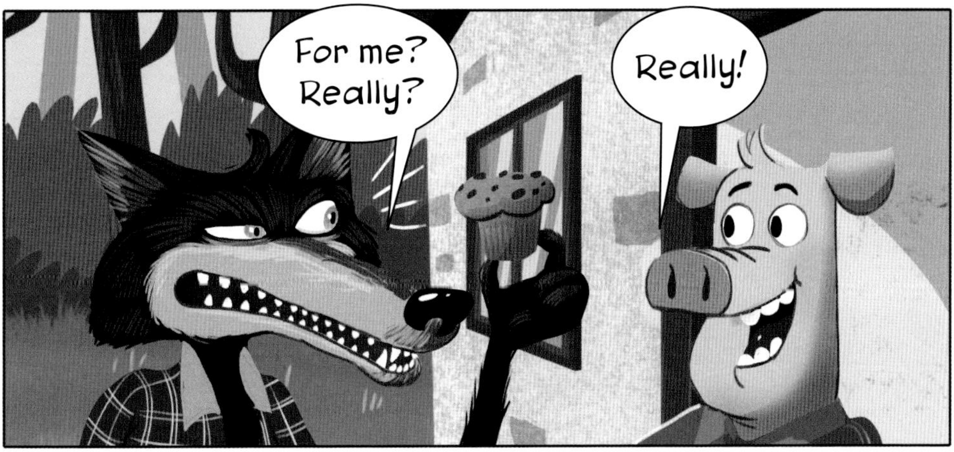
For me? Really?
Really!

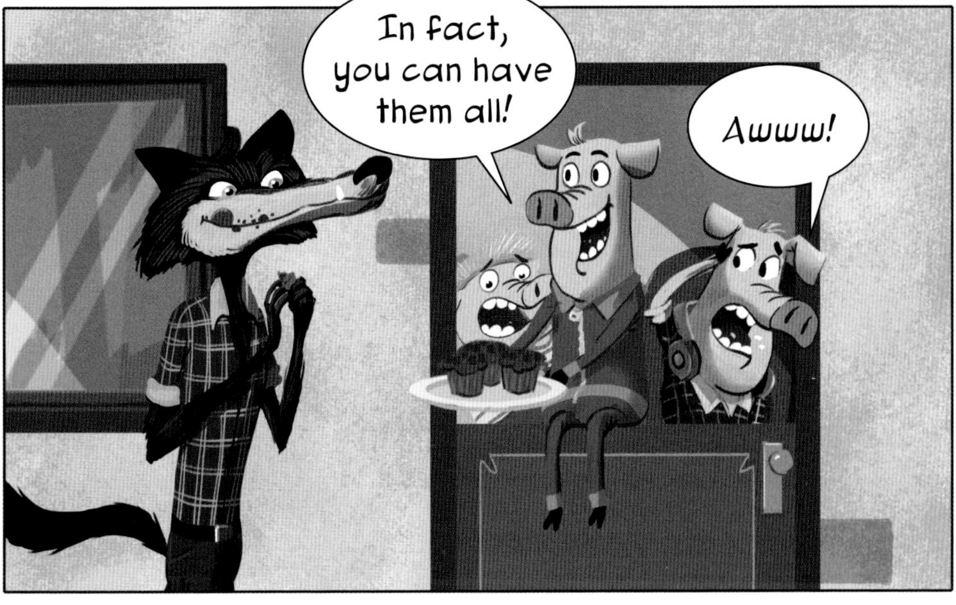
In fact, you can have them all!
Awww!

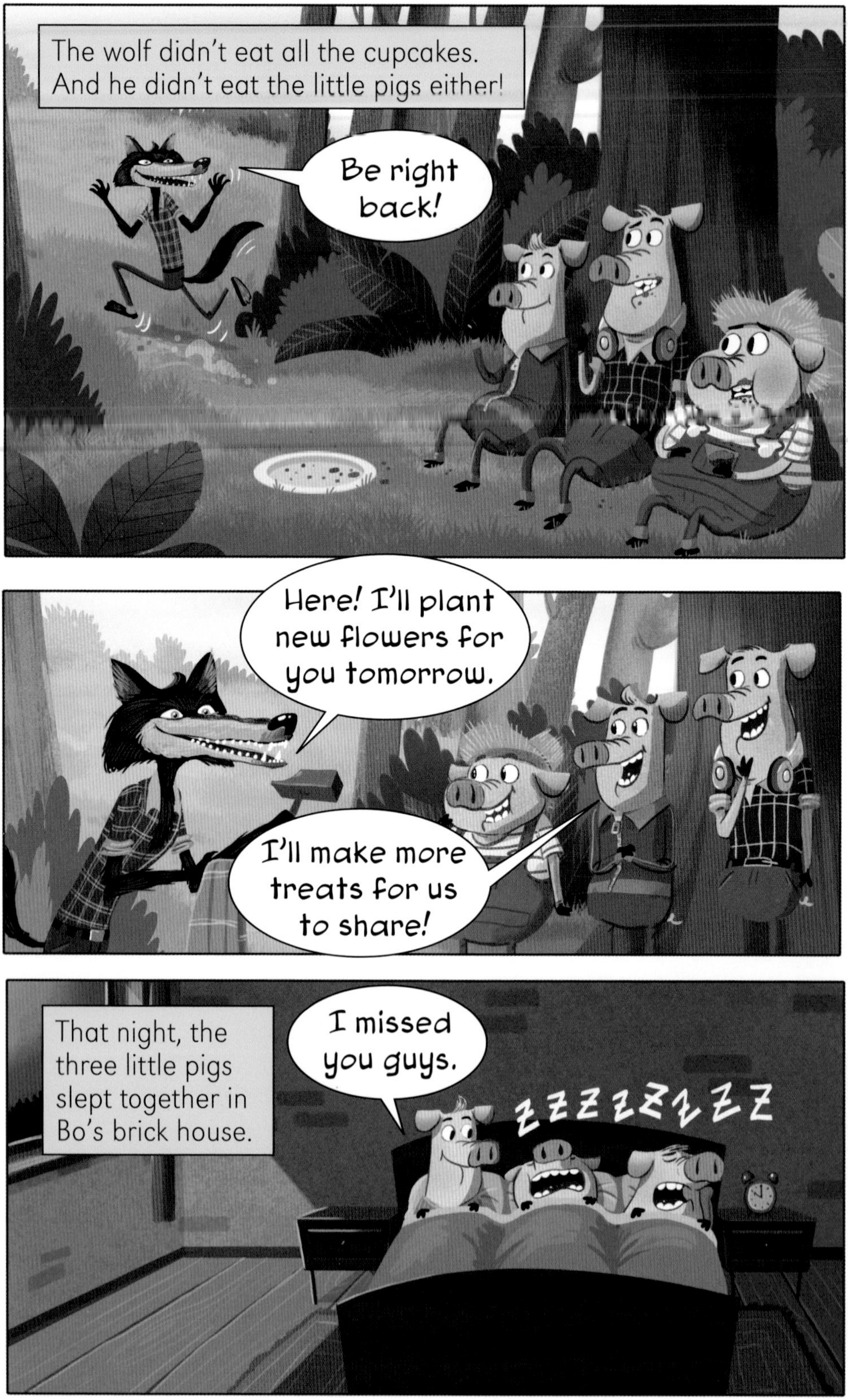
The wolf didn't eat all the cupcakes. And he didn't eat the little pigs either!
Be right back!
Here! I'll plant new flowers for you tomorrow.
I'll make more treats for us to share!
That night, the three little pigs slept together in Bo's brick house.
I missed you guys.
ZZZZZZZZ

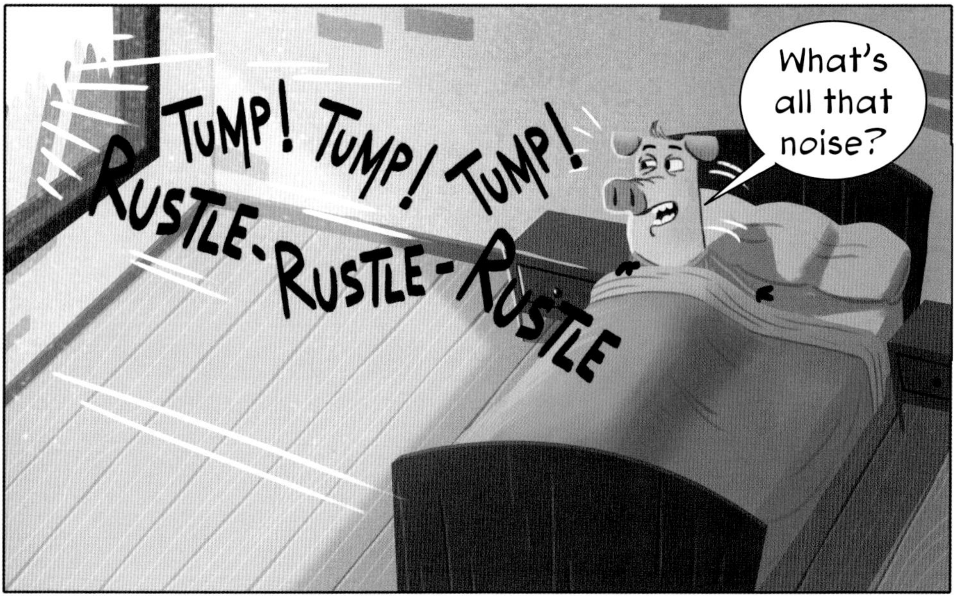
TUMP! TUMP! TUMP!
RUSTLE-RUSTLE-RUSTLE
What's all that noise?

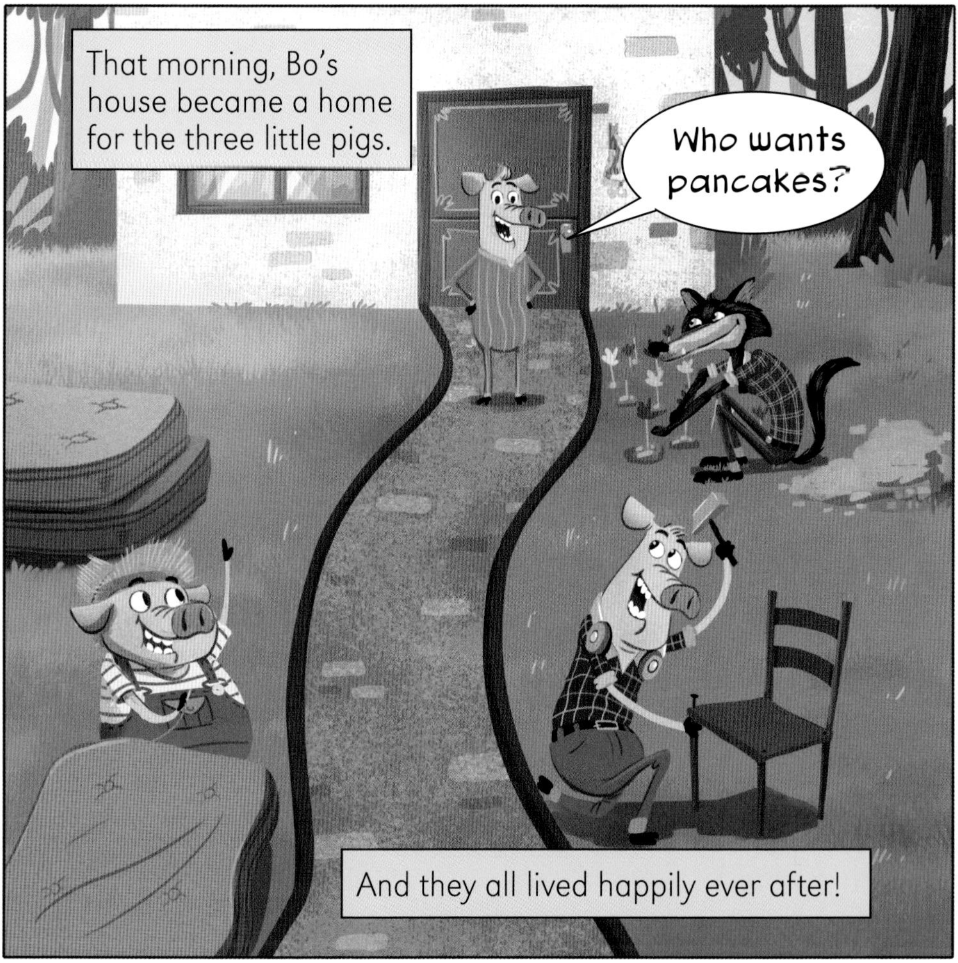
That morning, Bo's house became a home for the three little pigs.
Who wants pancakes?
And they all lived happily ever after!

WRITING PROMPTS

1. The big bad wolf is very hungry. Make a list of 10 foods that you eat. Circle your favorites!

2. Jem likes to sleep. What do you think he dreams about? Write a short paragraph that describes one of Jem's dreams.

3. The big bad wolf does not blow down the brick house. If he had blown it down, what might have happened next? Write a short story that tells the tale!

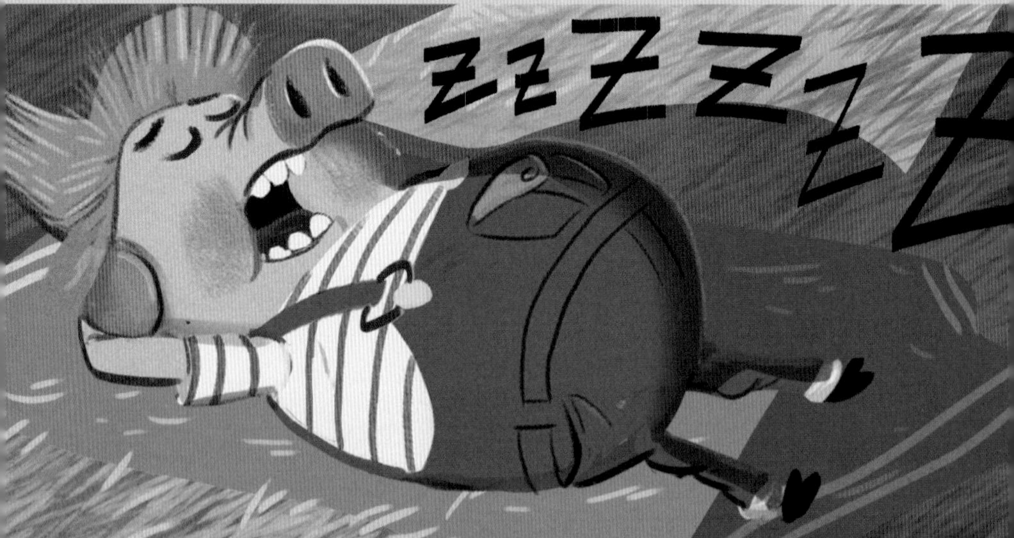
ZZZZZZZZ

DISCUSSION QUESTIONS

1. Clem and Jem are afraid of the big bad wolf. Talk to an adult about an animal that scares you and an animal that you love.

2. Jem thinks Clem will help him build his house. Clem doesn't help him. Do you think Clem should have helped Jem?

3. Bo is nice to the big bad wolf, and the wolf becomes his friend. Have you ever made a friend by doing something nice?

BUILD YOUR OWN STICK HOUSE

Clem built a house made of sticks. You can build a little stick house too!

WHAT YOU NEED:

- toothpicks
- mini-marshmallows, gumdrops, raisins, or other small, sticky treats

WHAT YOU DO:

1. Carefully push a sticky treat onto one end of a toothpick.

2. Poke another toothpick into the same sticky treat to make a straight line.

3. Repeat steps 1 and 2 three more times. You should have four straight lines.

4. Form the lines into a square and connect the corners with more sticky treats. You've just made the bottom of your house!

5. Now build walls and rooms by adding more toothpicks and treats. Make any shapes you want!

READ ALL THE AMAZING DISCOVER GRAPHICS BOOKS!

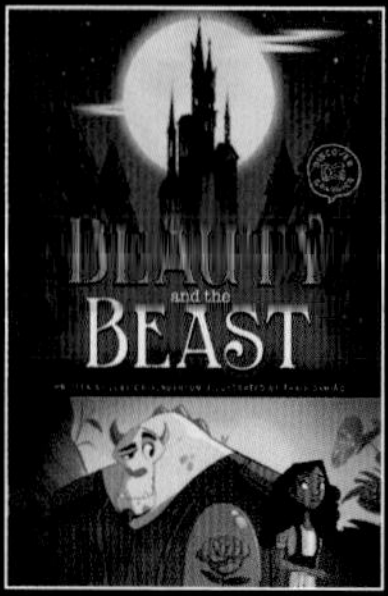
Beauty and the Beast

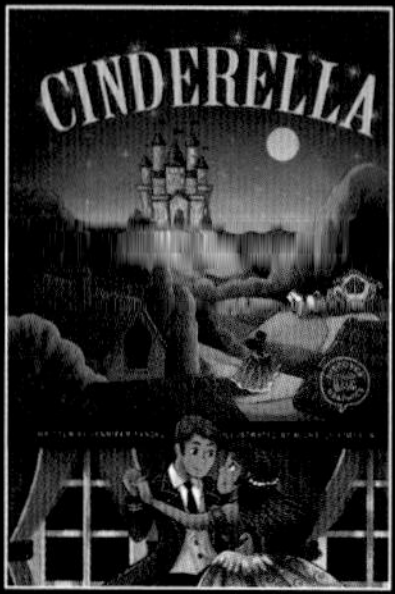
Cinderella

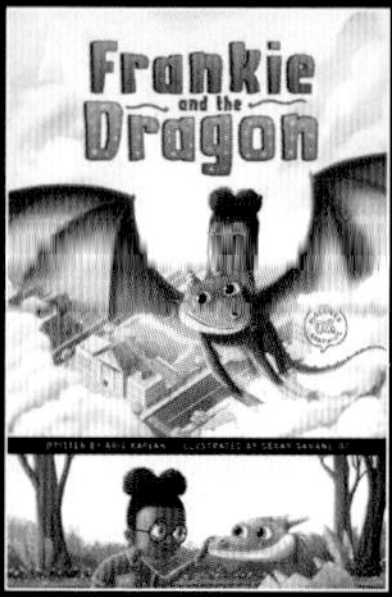
Frankie and the Dragon

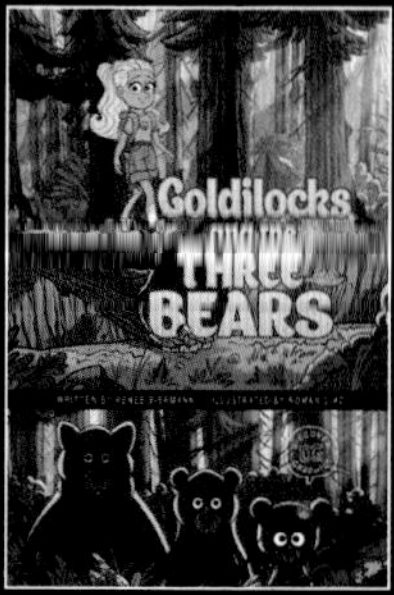
Goldilocks and the Three Bears

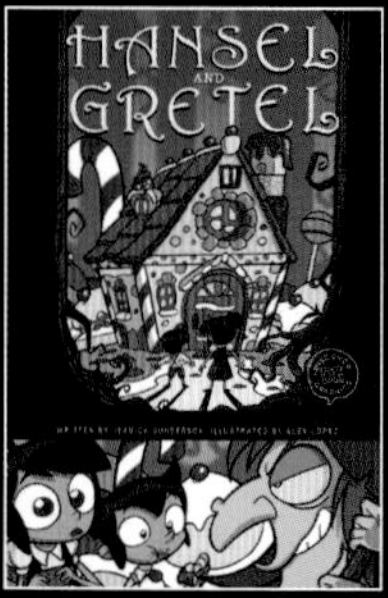
Hansel and Gretel

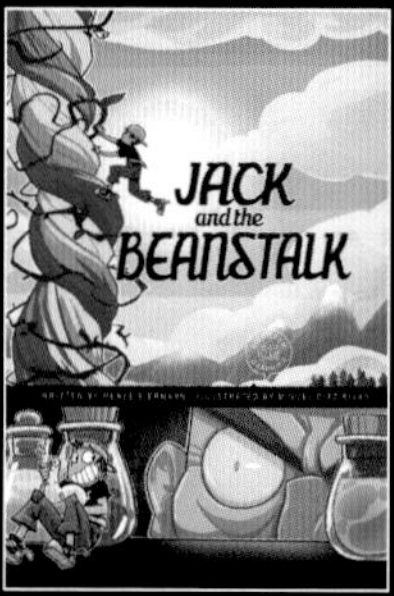
Jack and the Beanstalk

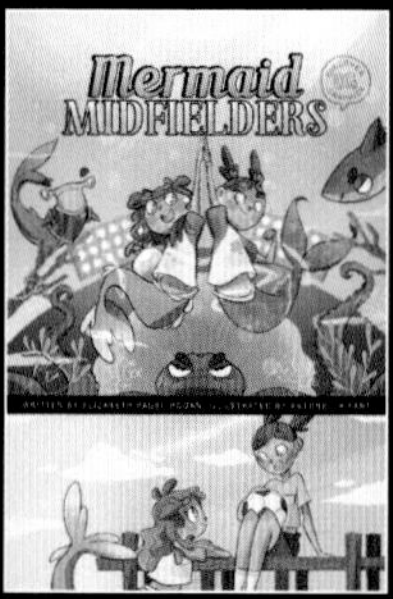
Mermaid Midfielders

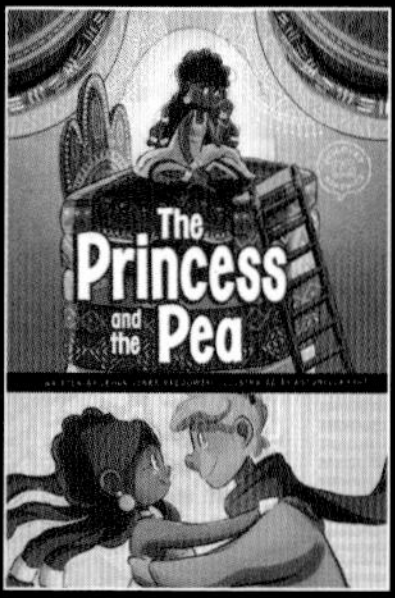
The Princess and the Pea

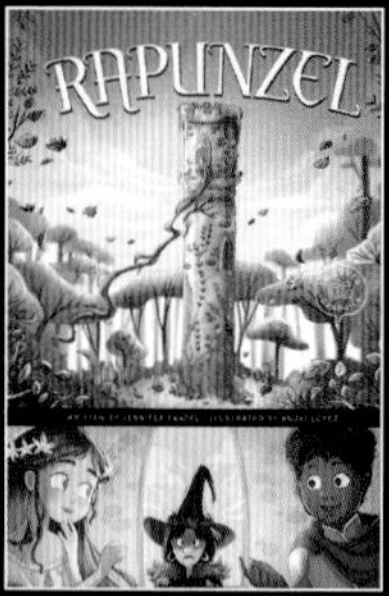
Rapunzel

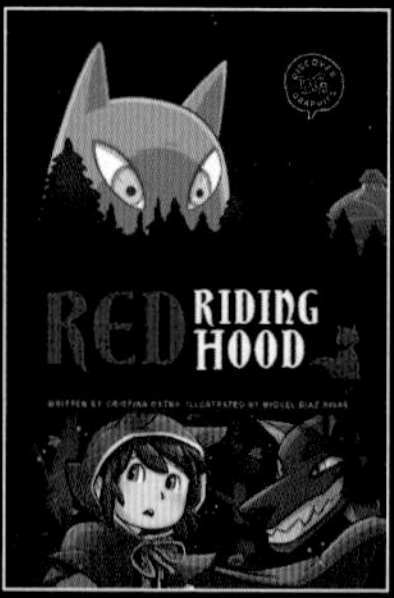
Red Riding Hood

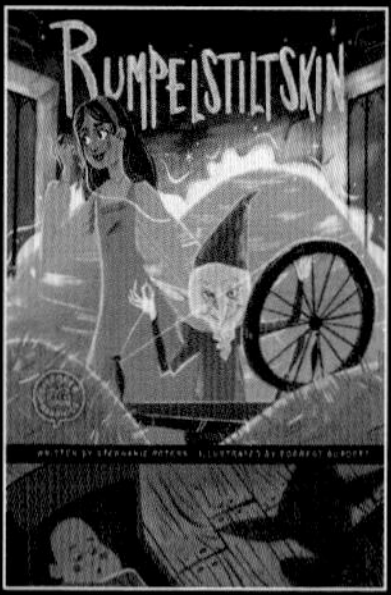
Rumpelstiltskin

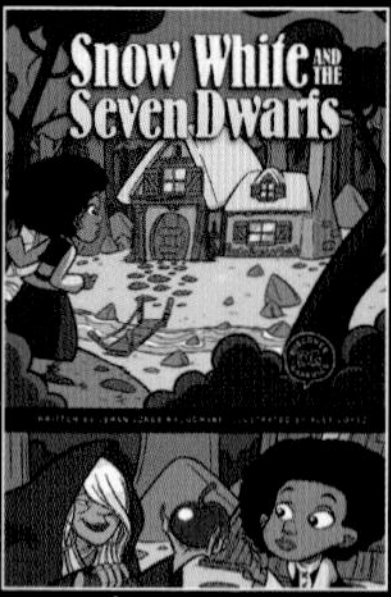
Snow White and the Seven Dwarfs

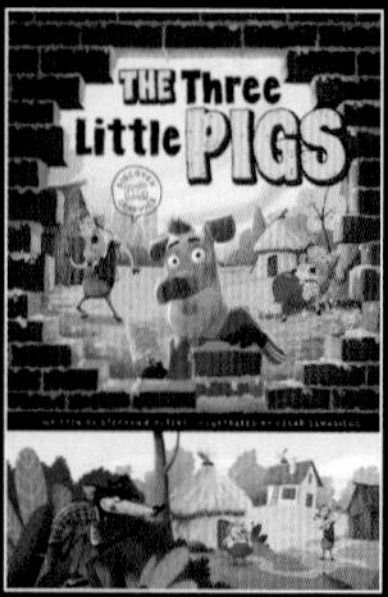
The Three Little Pigs

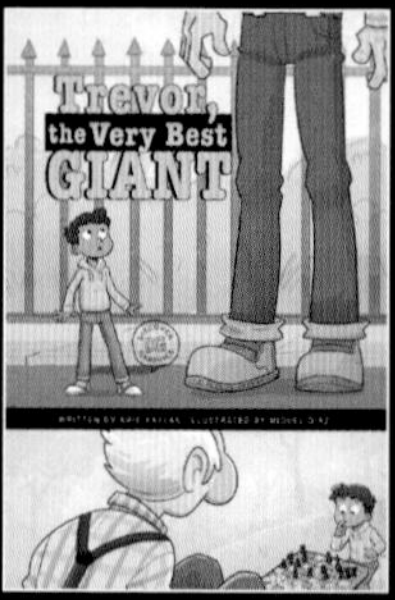
Trevor, the Very Best Giant

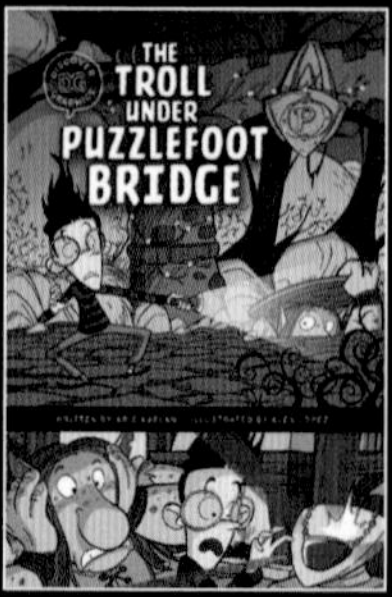
The Troll Under Puzzlefoot Bridge

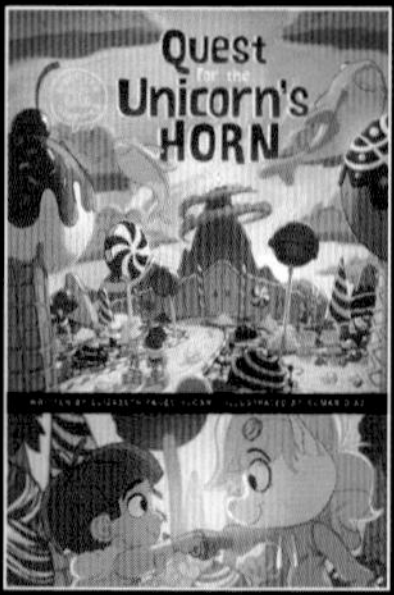
Quest for the Unicorn's Horn

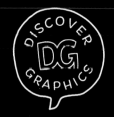